"Jennifer, why are we in the closet?"

Trevor chuckled when she closed the door, enveloping them in darkness.

"Can you see me?" she asked with a muffled giggle.

"No. It's dark in here."

"I know."

"So why are we in the closet?" he questioned again, his voice threaded with amusement.

"We're in here because of chickens and frogs, Trevor."

"Chickens and frogs? Jennifer, what in the world are you talking about?"

"That, Dr. Hawke," she purred, "is Dr. Jennifer Hamilton's version of the birds and the bees. You owe me a kiss. I'm here to collect."

Dear Reader,

Spellbinders! That's what we're striving for. The editors at Silhouette are determined to capture your imagination and win your heart with every single book we publish. Each month, six Special Editions are chosen with *you* in mind.

Our authors are our inspiration. Writers such as Nora Roberts, Tracy Sinclair, Kathleen Eagle, Carole Halston and Linda Howard—to name but a few—are masters at creating endearing characters and heartrending love stories. Their characters are everyday people—just like you and me—whose lives have been touched by love, whose dreams and desires suddenly come true!

So find a cozy, quiet place to read, and create your own special moment with a Silhouette Special Edition.

Sincerely,

The Editors
SILHOUETTE BOOKS

ALLYSON RYAN
Love Can Make It Better

Silhouette Special Edition

Published by Silhouette Books New York

America's Publisher of Contemporary Romance

With love to
Aunt Charlene, who gave me the courage to write;
Mom, for her unwavering love and support;
and Bob, my husband and real-life hero.

SILHOUETTE BOOKS
300 East 42nd St., New York, N.Y. 10017

Copyright © 1987 by Linda Kichline

ISBN: 0-373-09398-5

First Silhouette Books printing August 1987

America's Publisher of Contemporary Romance

Printed in the U.S.A.

ALLYSON RYAN

loves reading, people watching and traveling. Starting in Colorado and working her way across the country, she finally settled in Pennsylvania with her husband and their four beloved cats. She attributes sixteen years of marital bliss to her husband's uncanny ability to remember their anniversary—one day after the eldest cat's birthday.

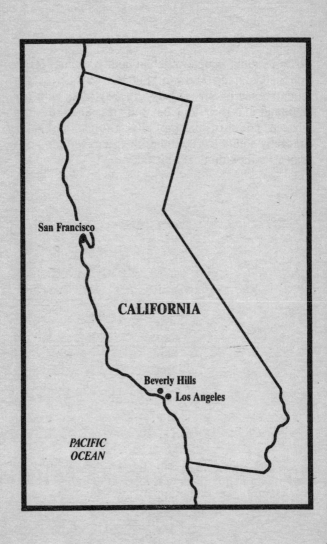

Chapter One

Dr. Trevor Hawke pulled his silver Mercedes to a stop at the curb in the unfamiliar, seedy neighborhood on the fringes of East Los Angeles and lifted a hand-drawn map. According to the directions, the alley directly ahead was the one he was seeking.

He looked up and warily studied the warehouses towering on either side of the alley. Complete with chain-link fences and gates secured with chains and padlocks, the buildings were more reminiscent of prison facilities than business establishments. A shiver raced up his spine when a snarling guard dog stepped from the shadows to stare at the car.

Trevor felt out of his element and for one brief moment considered turning the car around and driving home. But he dismissed the thought the instant he cast a glance toward his eight-year-old son. He'd walk through Hell to make Damien well, and this neighborhood, though unsavory, was still a far cry from that netherworld.

As if sensing his father's scrutiny, Damien glanced up and complained, "I don't like this place. Why did we come here?"

"Because there's a doctor here I need to see," Trevor explained. He pulled away from the curb. "It won't take long, Damien," he added as he turned the car into the alley.

"I want to go home," Damien announced, crossing his arms over his chest in an all too familiar mutinous gesture.

"We'll go home after I see the doctor," Trevor answered, directing an impatient glance at his son. "I expect you to behave—do you hear me?"

Damien's lower lip thrust out in a petulant pout, and Trevor heaved an inward sigh. The last thing he needed was for Damien to indulge in one of his infamous temper tantrums. It was going to be difficult enough to convince child psychologist Dr. Jennifer Hamilton to accept the boy as a patient.

The warehouses on either side of them blocked out the late-afternoon sun, and Trevor blinked when he spotted a golden burst of light ahead. The light at the end of the tunnel, he thought; then he shook his head in amusement at his own whimsy. As he drove from the dark cavern his eyes narrowed against the bright sunshine, then widened in surprise.

He'd driven into a large open area that fronted a small, brightly painted warehouse. A thriving garden sat at one end, and a crowd of teenagers with wild hairdos and even wilder attire was playing basketball on a cracked slab of pavement at the other end. They paused to eye the car curiously, then dismissed it and returned to their game.

"Would you like to come in, or would you like to wait in the car?" Trevor asked Damien as he braked to a stop in front of the warehouse. A gigantic orange sign above the door declared the building to be Hamilton House.

Damien nervously studied the surroundings. "I want to go with you."

"Fine."

Trevor climbed out, pocketed his keys and rounded the car. He opened the back door and removed the wheelchair, making certain it was secure before he lifted Damien's frail body out of the front seat and gently settled him into the chair. He stepped behind the wheelchair, and, as always, his heart wrenched as he stared down at his son's silken head. He looked so very tiny and vulnerable in the metal conveyance that had become a self-imposed prison.

A tall thin black girl of about sixteen approached them and smiled. Her hair was so closely cropped that if it hadn't been for the three earrings in each ear and the small rounded curves at the front of her T-shirt, Trevor would have had to perform a physical examination to determine her sex.

"Hi!" she greeted them cheerfully. "You here to see Jenny?"

"Yes," Trevor replied, returning her engaging smile. "I'm Dr. Hawke. I have an appointment."

"Jenny said to expect you," the girl said as she snapped her gum and lowered her dark-eyed gaze to Damien.

"This is my son, Damien."

"Hi, Damien." The girl bent down to Damien's eye level and extended her hand. Damien cautiously accepted it. "I'm Angel," she told him. "Would you like to help me referee the basketball game?"

"I don't know how to referee," Damien said, glancing over his shoulder to eye the game.

"It's not that hard. If you're interested, I'll teach you."

Damien glanced up at his father, and Trevor shrugged. "You can if you want. It's up to you."

The boy hesitated, then nodded, and Trevor stepped aside to let the girl assume his position behind the chair. She winked at him and said, "I have a kid sister like this."

Before Trevor could respond, she'd expertly pivoted the chair and was rolling Damien toward the makeshift basketball court. Trevor watched until the girl brought Damien to a stop and squatted beside him, talking and pointing. Damien seemed content, and with a relieved sigh, Trevor walked toward the front door of Hamilton House.

He'd just raised his hand to knock, when the door flew open and a tall lanky boy came barreling out.

"Oops! Sorry!" the boy apologized breathlessly when he collided with Trevor, almost sending them both sprawling.

Trevor stared at the boy in disbelief. His huge bush of hair looked as if he'd styled it by putting his finger into an electrical socket. One half had been dyed a shocking pink, the other half a vibrant orange.

The teenager gave him a sheepish grin. "I'm always in a hurry and running into something. That's why they call me 'Racer.' You must be Dr. Hawke," he said as his eyes moved skeptically over Trevor's hand-tailored three-piece suit. "Jenny's expecting you. Second door on the left. Just knock. She's re-potting Lady Greene. Sorry about running into you like that."

Trevor nodded and watched the boy race toward the basketball game. Cautiously he peered through the open door to make sure he wasn't in the path of an-other fast-moving teenager. Once he stepped inside, his gaze moved with interest around the hallway. It was evident that the interior of Hamilton House—a home for teenage runaways—had been expertly reno-vated. The cheerful hallway was immaculate, and an eclectic collection of prints and posters hung along its length.

A door stood open on his right, and a small sign nailed above it read: Community Room. Trevor re-sisted the urge to look in and moved down the hall-way in search of Dr. Jennifer Hamilton. A smile curved his lips when he arrived at the second door on the left. A hand-lettered sign taped to it announced:

Jennifer Anne Hamilton, Ph.D.
Child Psychologist Extraordinaire
Open 24 hours, 7 days a week
Knock twice and enter at your own risk

Jennifer hummed Tchaikovsky's *1812 Overture*, doing a fairly good imitation of the cannon shots as she poured the last of the potting soil into Lady Greene's new planter. She'd raised the avocado tree from a pit, and now it stood more than six feet high. She poured in a healthy amount of water and patted the soil down before standing to admire her handi-work. Tipping her head back to survey the top of the tree, she placed her hands on her hips, unconcerned about the muddy palm prints that now adorned her denim cutoffs. The tail of her faded cotton blouse was straggling out of her waistband, and the elastic securing her copper-colored hair had slipped, leaving her ponytail lopsided, too. She was a mess, but her tree looked terrific.

"You're looking good, Lady Greene," she informed the plant. "Let's get you back into your corner."

She bent down and began to struggle with the pot. "Come in!" she called out at the two quick raps on the door. When she heard it open, she said, "You arrived just in the nick of time! I need help moving Lady Greene."

Trevor chuckled softly as he eyed the young woman struggling with an enormous ceramic pot containing a sizable avocado tree. His gaze began at her small bare feet and traveled up a pair of shapely tanned legs, finally coming to rest on a delightfully rounded derriere that strained against the seams of a pair of muddy denim shorts so worn that they were almost white.

"That pot's bigger than you are," he announced.

Jennifer froze at the sound of the unfamiliar, husky baritone. Then she raised her right elbow and peered underneath it. Two man-size Italian loafers and an impressive pair of long legs clad in impeccably tailored navy suit pants were walking toward her.

"Uh-oh," she whispered when the shoes came to a stop beside her. She lowered her elbow and slowly raised her head, letting her eyes move appraisingly up the slacks and matching suit jacket and vest. "Three pieces, to boot," she muttered, then let her eyes move on up to a grinning, handsome face that took her breath away.

"Dr. Hamilton, I presume?" Trevor said with a chuckle. His grin widened as he watched her mud-smeared nose twitch as if she were trying to decide whether to laugh or to be annoyed. "Allow me," he said, easily lifting the pot, Lady Greene and all. "Where does it go?"

"In the corner next to the window," Jennifer answered, and watched him relocate the pot. "It must be nice to have muscles," she said with an envious sigh.

He turned toward her and smiled. "It comes in handy at times. You *are* Dr. Hamilton, aren't you?"

"Guilty as charged." She laughed. "And you're Dr. Hawke, right?"

"Right, but let's do away with the formalities. Call me Trevor, and I'll call you Jennifer, if that's okay."

"I'll go along with that." She extended her hand, then withdrew it immediately as she spotted the coating of potting soil. She chuckled and grinned up at him. "We'll skip the amenities, too, unless you're into mud pies. Please have a seat." She waved toward a chair beside her desk. "If you don't mind, I'll run down the hall and wash my hands. I'll only be a minute."

"Take your time. I'm in no rush," he told her while studying the delicate lines of her face. Her hazel eyes were almond shaped and framed by thick fringes of long copper lashes. With her ponytail askew and her face smudged with dirt, she looked more like a mischievous little girl than a thirty-two-year-old child psychologist with an extraordinary success record in the treatment of troubled youth. He was studying her so intently that an involuntary flush spread across her cheeks and she lowered her head shyly.

"I'll be right back," she said as she turned and walked toward the door, resisting the urge to race from the room. His candid scrutiny had set off an internal alarm system and had made her pulse pick up speed.

Good heavens, what was wrong with her? she wondered impatiently. All the man had done was look at her—and she'd done a little looking of her own. But it was the *way* he'd looked at her, she admitted as she hurried down the hallway and into the half bath. It had been the look of a man assessing a woman. The most disturbing part was that for the first time since her husband's death she'd responded.

Her brows drew together in a contemplative frown as she washed her hands and wondered why *the* Dr. Trevor Hawke, the only son of wealthy business entrepreneur Reginald Hawke, had come to see her. When Dr. Edward Markham, a mutual friend and the chief of staff of an exclusive private sanitarium in Los Angeles, had called and asked her to meet with Trevor Hawke, she'd agreed. Edward was not only a close friend, but also her mentor and staunchest supporter in the creation of Hamilton House. She'd have agreed to meet King Kong in a dark alley at midnight if Edward had asked her to, but she'd probably have more in common with King Kong than she did with the Beverly Hills cardiac surgeon waiting in her office, she thought wryly.

She glanced into the mirror and groaned when she saw the mud smeared across her face and her disheveled hair. What a way to make an impression! She grabbed a washcloth, scrubbed her face, resecured the ponytail and walked out of the bath. As she paused to tuck her blouse back into the waistband of her soiled shorts, her alert ears picked up the sound of conspiratorial whispering. A laugh escaped her when she crossed to the hall closet, threw open the door and two young boys fell out. They were both short and pudgy and dressed identically. The kids called them Pete and Re-Pete, but Jennifer always thought of them as Tweedledee and Tweedledum.

"What are you two up to?"

"Nothing, Jenny!" one youth exclaimed innocently.

"Yeah, Jenny, we're not doing nothing!" the other affirmed.

"We're not doing *anything*," Jennifer automatically corrected as she leaned into the closet and confiscated a small white cube from the floor. "We don't play craps at Hamilton House, guys, and you know it. Give me the other die."

"The other what?"

"The mate to this," Jennifer answered, holding up the single to a pair of dice.

"I wonder how that got in there," one boy said in awe.

"Yeah, I wonder how that got in there," the other mimicked.

Jennifer chuckled and pocketed the cube. "I guess it must be the egg-hatching season for dice. Before you know it, we'll have all kinds of these little creatures all over the house and I'll have to call the exterminator. Why don't you two go outside and get some fresh air?"

"It's too hot out there, Jenny."

"Yeah, Jenny, it's an *oven* out there."

She tapped a finger against her lips as if giving their complaints careful thought. "All right. If you want to stay inside, you can make yourselves useful by helping Theresa and Sundance bake bread."

"On second thought, I really do need some fresh air!"

"Yeah, me, too!"

The two boys scrambled to their feet, tore down the hallway and out the front door, the threat of kitchen duty hot on their heels.

Jennifer glanced up in surprise when a deep, rumbling chuckle echoed down the hallway. Trevor was leaning against the doorframe of her office, his coat-tails thrown back and his hands in his pockets. Jennifer's gaze was magnetically drawn to the front of his slacks, where the fabric stretched intimately across his flat abdomen. Little X-rated visions began to dance through her head, and with a gulp, she jerked her head up. Now just where had those naughty visions come from?

"Egg-hatching season for dice?" Trevor questioned in amusement, his eyes narrowing as he watched another stain of color wash her cheeks. He'd been perfectly aware of the direction of her scrutiny a moment before, and an unexpected surge of desire erupted in the pit of his stomach. His own cheeks now slightly flushed, he pushed impatiently away from the doorframe. He'd come here to convince the woman to help Damien, not to indulge in romantic fantasies.

Jennifer shrugged and strolled toward him. "If the boys didn't put it in the closet, I don't know how else it got there." She pulled the small cube from her pocket and tossed it to him. "Take it with you. Maybe you can use it for medical research. If I keep it, it will mysteriously disappear.''

Trevor caught the flying cube and dropped it into his pocket before stepping aside to let Jennifer precede him back into her office. His nostrils flared as she passed and a delicate, elusive fragrance drifted toward him. As if on command, his eyes dropped to follow the natural, provocative sway of her hips as she walked in front of him. Another, more intense surge of desire assaulted him as his eyes moved lower to her long bare legs. He had an almost irresistible urge to touch them.

He sucked in a deep breath and closed his eyes. There was no way he was going to become involved with this woman. They had about as much in common as a desert and a tropical forest.

But that wasn't exactly true, he reminded himself, opening his eyes and letting his gaze wander over her lush figure one last time. She was the heir to the O'Brien fortune. Like him, she'd been born and raised with a silver spoon in her mouth. Unlike him, she'd walked away from all the privileges her money offered. Why?

It was an intriguing question, and Trevor realized it had been a long time since he'd been intrigued by a woman. The thought caused him to shift his shoulders uncomfortably beneath his suit jacket. He had a feeling that something significant was happening here, and he wasn't certain he liked it.

Jennifer crossed to her desk and settled into the wobbly typing chair behind it. Her eyes drifted over Trevor as she watched him take a seat. He sported the well-toned, muscled grace of a man who worked out in a gym on a regular basis. His mink-brown hair curled over the tops of his ears and hung unfashionably long over the collar of his white shirt. It had been carefully brushed back, but errant wisps defied taming and spiraled rakishly over his broad forehead. Dark brows were bold slashes over startling violet eyes fringed with long, spiky lashes. His features were aquiline with a hint of aristocracy, a sure sign of his wealthy background. His mobile mouth was curved into a smile, one corner tilted slightly higher than the other, as he sat casually relaxed beneath her inspection.

Jennifer felt something elemental stir inside and quickly clamped it down. Dr. Trevor Hawke represented everything she'd fought so hard to escape. There was no way she could become involved with him. Absolutely no way at all.

"So what can I do for you, Trevor?" she asked, frowning at the breathless quality of her voice.

His smile faded, and his eyes darkened with worry. "I came to talk to you about my son."

"I see." She gently asked, "Is your son a runaway?"

"No. Damien was in a car accident a year ago. His mother was killed, and he suffered a spinal injury that required extensive surgery. He's been confined to a wheelchair ever since."

"I'm very sorry," Jennifer said sincerely, deeply touched by his forlorn expression.

Trevor nodded and said hoarsely. "Thank you." He paused to clear his throat before continuing. "Anyway, Damien's surgery was successful, but he's convinced himself that he still can't walk, and refuses to cooperate with his physical therapist. He suffers from bouts of severe depression and uncontrollable rages."

A rueful smile curved his lips. " 'Temper tantrums' is a more accurate description."

Jennifer gave a sage nod. "An accident like that is very emotionally traumatic, and anger is a normal response. How old is Damien?"

"He just turned eight. I'm afraid he blames himself for his mother's death."

Jennifer's hand tightened around the pencil she'd picked up as a flash of memory hit her. Flames were shooting toward the sky, and she was being thrown. Water engulfed her, and she was being sucked down and down and down. Then she was flying upward, and there was an explosion and— She shook her head to bring herself back to the present.

"He's confessed his feelings of guilt?"

"Yes," Trevor answered, wondering why she'd suddenly paled. "According to Damien, a small dog ran in front of the car. Patricia didn't see it, and Damien grabbed the steering wheel. Evidently Patricia lost control of the car, and it went over a cliff. She was killed instantly."

Tears clouded Jennifer's eyes, and she glanced down at her desk to hide them. "Has Damien been in counseling?"

"From the beginning, but I'm afraid he's resisting treatment. No one has been able to reach him. Quite frankly, Jennifer, I'm at my wit's end, and I don't know where to turn. If I don't get him back on his feet soon, his leg muscles will begin to atrophy, and he'll be handicapped for the rest of his life."

Jennifer nodded in understanding and looked up at him with a consoling smile. "It's been a terribly difficult year for you, too. I hope you haven't been too proud to seek a little counseling of your own."

"I haven't. Edward's been a good friend of mine for years, and he's always there when I need to talk."

"Edward's one of the best psychiatrists in the country," she stated unnecessarily, and then gave a confused shake of her head. "I don't understand why you came to me, Trevor. If you're seeking the name of a counselor, I'll be glad to recommend a few, but Edward would have a better idea of who's qualified to help your son. The psychiatrists and psychologists I deal with specialize mostly in the treatment of runaways."

"Actually, Edward recommended that I try to convince you to take Damien's case."

"Me?" she said in disbelief. "Why would Edward recommend me?" But even as she asked the question, a little voice deep inside provided the answer. She and Damien shared a common ground. He'd accidentally killed his mother. She'd accidentally killed her father. "I treat runaways, Trevor," she stated firmly. "I'm neither trained nor qualified to treat your son."

"That's not true," Trevor countered. "You've had phenomenal success in treating troubled youth, and I can't think of a better description than troubled for Damien." He leaned forward and placed his elbows on her desk as if to add emphasis to his words. "You've managed to reach kids the system had branded as hopeless. After talking with Edward and reviewing your record, I'm convinced that you and only you can reach Damien. Help me, Jennifer. He's my only child, and I'm losing him. I need your help."

Jennifer slowly released her breath and leaned back in her chair in an effort to place some distance between them. His plea was heartbreaking. She couldn't stand to see any child hurting, but how could she fit

Damien Hawke into her schedule? Trevor could afford a team of the best doctors in the country. Her charges at Hamilton House depended on her and her alone. She couldn't take time away from them to help Damien Hawke. She just couldn't. She glanced away from those big pleading violet eyes. Violet eyes should look ridiculous on a man, so why didn't they look ridiculous on him?

"I'm sorry, Trevor, but I can't help you." She sighed regretfully. "My days at Hamilton House are full, and it would be impossible for me to come to your home and spend the necessary time with Damien on a routine basis. Like you, I have only twenty-four hours in a day, and I'm sorely taxing those hours as it is."

Trevor shifted nervously in his chair. "Actually, I was thinking more along the lines of having Damien move into Hamilton House."

"Move in?" Jennifer echoed incredulously. She gave a firm shake of her head. "That's even more impossible. The kids here range in age from thirteen to seventeen. Damien is eight. He wouldn't have anyone in his age group to associate with. Then there's the complication of his wheelchair. All our bedrooms are on the second floor, and there isn't an elevator. The stairs are much too narrow and dangerous to try to maneuver him up and down them. We'd have to work out some kind of sleeping arrangement on the first floor, and he'd be even more isolated. Isolation is the last thing Damien needs at this point."

When Trevor looked unconvinced, she concluded with, "Trevor, I also have a problem of overcrowding. There are twenty teenagers at Hamilton House right now, and I have only one assistant. That's ten teenagers per adult. Surely you can see that our hands are full.''

"Then you refuse to help him," he stated wearily.

"I'm very sorry," Jennifer replied. "If I even remotely felt I could devote the attention to Damien that he needs, I'd give it a try. But my kids have to come first, and moving Damien into Hamilton House wouldn't be fair to him, to the kids already here or to me and my assistant. Can you understand that?''

He nodded. "Yes. You have kids hanging from the rafters. The last thing you need to cope with is a little boy confined to a wheelchair when he shouldn't be."

"That was an awfully low blow, Dr. Hawke."

He gave her a weak smile. "It didn't work, huh?"

"It didn't work," she answered with a weak smile of her own. "But I will make some calls and see if I can't come up with the name of a good counselor. Deal?''

"I suppose I don't have any choice," he answered with a resigned sigh, and rose to his feet. "Thank you for your time, Jennifer."

"I really am sorry I couldn't help," she told him as she also stood.

"I do understand your problems," he assured her, extending his hand across the desk.

Jennifer marveled at its strength and its warmth as she accepted it. It was a nicely shaped hand with long, blunt-tipped fingers and fastidiously manicured nails. An errant vision of those hands sliding over her in a passionate exploration skittered through her mind, and she immediately jerked her hand back as if she'd been burned. She'd never had something like that happen in her life!

A sardonic smile touched Trevor's lips when she raised wide, questioning eyes to his face. He'd also felt the undeniable attraction and almost told her so, but he decided against it. As he'd determined before, he was here to seek her help, not to indulge in romantic fantasies, and he still had to play the last card in his hand. If she said no, he'd be defeated. If she said yes? Well, if she said yes, he might indulge in a few romantic fantasies.

But what in the world was it about her that he found so attractive? he wondered as he studied her face. Something in her eyes, he decided. Before he could decipher what that something was, she again ducked her head shyly, but it quickly shot up when he asked, "Would you like to meet Damien? He's outside."

Jennifer felt her heart begin to sink toward her toes. "Damien's here?"

"I take him with me whenever I can. As a surgeon, I don't have a lot of free time, and I try not to take any more of it away from him than I absolutely have to."

"That's very commendable. I'd be happy to meet him."

"Great. You can walk me out to my car."

Reluctantly Jennifer went with him. She didn't really relish the idea of meeting Damien Hawke. It was much easier to refuse help to an unknown face than a known one. But she had to say no, she thought, resolutely stiffening her spine. She couldn't run Hamilton House, treat Damien Hawke and still get an adequate night's sleep.

"There's my son," Trevor announced proudly as he swung open the front door and let Jennifer exit ahead of him. "I haven't seen him enjoying himself like this since the accident."

All the air rushed out of Jennifer's lungs, and she leaned weakly against the building. Damien was sitting in his wheelchair on the perimeter of a wild basketball game, shrilly blowing a whistle and waving his arms excitedly while the players argued good-naturedly with him about his call of a foul.

Sunlight glistened off his mink-brown hair—a shade and style identical to his father's. Jennifer's gaze drifted over him, taking in the miniature three-piece suit and glistening loafers that also mimicked his father's. When Trevor moved toward his son, Jennifer automatically followed.

"Damien, it's time to go home."

"But I don't want to go!" the boy protested, turning pleading eyes on his father. "Can't I stay a little longer? Please?"

"Not today. If Dr. Hamilton doesn't mind, maybe you can come back for another visit."

"Who's Dr. Hamilton?" Damien questioned, glancing around in search of an unfamiliar face.

When a pair of large violet eyes centered in a pale, boyish face landed on her, Jennifer glanced toward the sky in search of divine guidance.

"Are you Dr. Hamilton?" he asked.

"Yes, but you may call me Jenny," Jennifer answered, extending her hand. He accepted it and gave it a formal shake.

"I'm pleased to meet you, Jenny," he said very correctly. Then he eagerly asked, "Can I come back to play? Is it all right?"

"You're welcome at Hamilton House anytime, Damien."

"Thank you." He carefully removed the whistle from around his neck, handed it to Angel and told her, "Thank you for teaching me how to referee, Angel."

"You're welcome, kid." She pressed the whistle back into his hand. "Take it home and practice so you'll be ready to take over when you come back for a visit."

"Really?" Damien asked, his eyes widening until they almost encompassed his face. "Is it all right, Dad?"

"It's all right, Damien."

"Wow!" he exclaimed in excitement, clenching the whistle tightly. "This is the best present I've ever had!"

Trevor glanced toward Jennifer as he placed his hands on the back of the wheelchair and dryly said, "And Santa spends a fortune every Christmas."

Jennifer chuckled. "Sometimes it's the little things that are the most important."

"I suppose you're right."

Jennifer and a crowd of teenagers accompanied Trevor and Damien to the car and stood beside it while Trevor settled Damien inside, folded the wheelchair and placed it in the back. He closed the door and turned toward Jennifer while reaching into the breast pocket of his suit jacket. He pulled out a business card and handed it to her.

"If you come up with the name of a counselor, give me a call."

"I will," she said, an involuntary shiver racing down her spine as their fingers brushed and those violet eyes once again roamed over her face. She knew she was in trouble when her gaze dropped to his sculptured lips and she imagined them pressing against her own. She forced her eyes back up to his and decided she'd definitely been a widow for much too long.

He nodded, rounded the car and slid in behind the steering wheel. The powerful engine roared to life, but before the car had a chance to move, Damien's window lowered. His small face was positively glowing as he peered out at the crowd.

"Dad says we can come next Saturday!" he informed them.

"Hey, that's great!" Angel exclaimed.

"Yeah!" Racer laughed and tossed an arm around Jennifer's shoulders. "Come early, and then the old slave driver here will have to let us out to play even if our chores aren't done."

Jennifer chuckled as she glanced up at the teenager. "You think so, huh?"

He leaned down and dropped a loud, exuberant kiss on her cheek. "Yeah. It's called company manners, and if I haven't learned anything else at good old H.H., I've learned my company manners."

"I'm glad to hear that," Jennifer responded with a laugh, wrapping her arm around the boy's waist.

Trevor backed the car slowly down the alley. He smiled and waved at Jennifer just before the car disappeared into the shadows of the other warehouses. She nodded and waved back, her gaze shifting from Trevor to the miniature of him at his side.

"Damn you, Edward Markham," she muttered. "You set me up. You told him to bring Damien because you knew if I saw him, I'd have to take him in. Someday I'm going to strangle you—if I don't kill you first."

Chapter Two

Jennifer sat at her desk and stewed after the Hawkes left Hamilton House. She'd been set up, and she knew it, but she kept seeing Trevor Hawke's pleading violet eyes and his son's pale little face. Her eyes drifted over the mountain of paperwork in front of her and then to the blueprints for her new, countrified Hamilton House, tacked to the wall.

Between her counseling schedule, the day-to-day activities of Hamilton House, and the construction site, there were too few hours in a day. She'd have to be crazy to take Damien in. He'd not only demand a lot of time, he'd also have to be carefully watched and supervised. An eight-year-old boy couldn't be given the same freedom the other kids enjoyed.

Restless, she rose from her chair and crossed to the framed photograph that sat on the scratched and dented file cabinet. Her father stood on the deck of the sailboat *Jenny*, the captain's hat she'd given him for Christmas tilted jauntily on his head, his lips curved in a wide grin. The picture had been taken one week before the accident that had claimed his life. The accident that had been her fault.

The feelings that rushed through her were bittersweet and laced with love and guilt. They were feelings that would remain with her throughout her life. They were feelings that Damien shared. With an impatient sigh, she turned away from the photo, crossed back to her desk and lifted the telephone receiver. After determining Edward Markham's schedule for the day from his receptionist, she grabbed her car keys and headed out the door.

Dr. Edward Markham resembled a cross between an imperious statesman and a mad concert pianist. His flowing white hair was in its usual disarray, and his bushy white brows were arched in surprise when Jennifer marched into his office two hours after the Hawkes had left Hamilton House. She was determined to make the most of the ten minutes Edward had between patients.

"Why, Jennifer, what a surprise!" Edward greeted her jovially.

"Surprise, my foot," she grumbled as she dropped into the chair in front of his desk and glared at him. "You set me up."

"Me?" he questioned in mock innocence.

"You knew if I saw that boy I'd have to take him in."

"Are we talking about Damien Hawke?"

"You know perfectly well that we are. Why did you send the Hawkes to me, Edward?"

He leaned back in his chair and cradled his hands beneath his chin. "Why ask a question you already know the answer to?"

"I buried my guilt, Edward. I have no desire to resurrect it."

"I'm not asking you to resurrect it, Jennifer. I'm asking you to help the boy."

"Edward, I am not professionally qualified to help that boy, and you know it."

"He's no different than your runaways."

"He is, too."

"Do you really believe that?"

"No."

He grinned at her irritated expression. "What are your real objections to taking on the case?"

That if his father hangs around Hamilton House I'll become a fallen woman, she thought melodramatically. Aloud she said, "Where am I going to find the time? I'm counseling twenty teenagers, Edward. Now you want me to take in an eight-year-old boy in a wheelchair. Do you have any idea how much time he'll need? We're talking about hours and hours a day!"

"No, we're not," Edward disagreed. "You know as well as I do that an hour or two a day and a little supervision is all you'll have to devote to him if he lives at Hamilton House. We'd only be talking hours and hours if you didn't have him in residence."

"*You* recommended that he live at Hamilton House!" she exclaimed, eyeing him accusingly.

"Yes, I did," Edward admitted without remorse. "We're talking about a young boy whose father's profession is extremely demanding. Damien lives in a mansion with a couple of servants and won't leave the house unless it's with his father. He refuses to go to school because some kids made fun of his wheelchair, so Trevor indulged him and hired a tutor. He needs exposure to people, Jenny, and not just servants who fear they might lose their jobs if they rock the boat. He needs someone who's been where he's been and is ready to kick him back into line. Do you understand what I'm saying?''

"Yes," Jennifer answered reluctantly, and closed her eyes. Immediately, Trevor Hawke's forlorn expression formed in her mind's eye, and she cursed inwardly. Damn him and those big violet eyes, anyway. He was probably blaming himself for Damien's reluctance to get well. Why couldn't she get him out of her mind? "What you're telling me is that Damien needs what I didn't get."

"Exactly," Edward responded. "You know as well as I do that one of the reasons you're so successful with those kids of yours is that they know you were a runaway and they accept you as one of them. I've often wondered if you would have done something as drastic as running away if I'd been able to find a Jennifer Hamilton to help you. I believe that you can succeed with Damien where others have failed because you can identify with him. At least it's worth a try, don't you think?''

"Probably." Jennifer sighed. "But what about his father?"

"What about him?"

"How is he going to handle all this? After all, I'm going to be taking his only child and doing only heaven knows what with him. I get the impression Trevor is rather protective of Damien, and I'm not certain I want to butt heads with him.''

Inwardly she admitted that what she'd like to do with the man had nothing to do with his son. Since her husband's death, Trevor was the first man to ever spark feelings of desire in her, and she frowned at that admission. Why Trevor Hawke?

"'Rather protective' is an understatement," Edward muttered. "I think Trevor is shooting for both Father and Mother of the Year with Damien. If Damien says jump, Trevor asks how high and how often.

"Jennifer, things were not very stable in Trevor's marriage when the accident occurred. In fact, Trevor and Patricia had been discussing divorce. In my opinion, they never should have married in the first place. Patricia was a lovely woman from a very wealthy background. She wanted a rich husband and the jet-set life-style she was accustomed to. She thought she'd found that when she married Reginald Hawke's son and heir apparent. Unfortunately for Patricia, Trevor is a dedicated physician. So what Patricia got was a very wealthy, very dedicated and, for her, very boring doctor for a husband. The only thing that held them together was their adoration of Damien. Now that she's gone and Trevor sees what Damien's going through, I think he's feeling guilty for ever considering divorce, and because of Damien's condition, he's overcompensating."

"How different from my own marriage," Jennifer said, smiling sadly.

"Yes, how very different," Edward agreed. "You and Tom were a rare couple, Jenny. But enough of that. Are you going to take Damien as a patient?"

"Do monkeys eat bananas?" Jennifer asked as she rose from the chair and settled her purse over her shoulder.

That evening, she arrived at the Hawke mansion in Beverly Hills twenty minutes earlier than her scheduled appointment. It hadn't been by design, however. She'd allowed herself extra time to deal with traffic, and traffic had been lighter than she'd anticipated.

At first she decided to wait in the car until the appointed time, but then she decided against it. Twenty minutes was twenty minutes. They were having a general meeting at Hamilton House tonight, and it was going to be a long one, since she planned on giving her infamous lecture on the chickens and the frogs.

She grinned at the thought as she climbed out of her twelve-year-old, rust-encrusted Chevy and strolled up the Hawke drive. The chickens and the frogs was her interpretation of the birds and the bees. Having twenty teenagers ranging in age from thirteen to seventeen and the boys outnumbering the girls two to one meant she had to keep a careful watch on their activities. She never tried to inhibit their natural drives but tried to teach them how to control them. So far, she'd been successful. Now if she could only practice what she preached and convince herself that the sexy Dr. Trevor Hawke was off-limits, she'd be in good shape.

What was it about him that she found so incredibly appealing? she wondered irritably as she followed the lushly landscaped path to the front door and rang the bell. He was everything she'd walked away from. A man born to wealth and happy to coexist with it—although happy was not quite true at this point in time, she had to admit. Money didn't buy everything, and it certainly hadn't bought him Damien's health or a happy marriage.

The front door swung open, and Jennifer arched a brow at the childish screaming she heard in the background. The housekeeper grimaced and raised a hand to her ear as the volume of the screaming increased. When it dropped a decibel, she said, "May I help you?"

"I'm Dr. Hamilton. I have an appointment with Dr. Hawke, but I'm a little early."

The housekeeper nodded and stepped back, gesturing for Jennifer to enter. Jennifer stepped across the threshold and let her gaze wander around the foyer. She'd always been a lover of art, and the paintings adorning the walls were worth a king's ransom. But mixed among the expensive oils were a few paintings in an unfamiliar style that reached out and touched all her emotions. She glanced down at the corner of one and took note of a boldly scrawled initial *T*. She wanted to explore the unfamiliar artist's work further, but the housekeeper's voice stopped her.

"I'll wait a few minutes before I tell Dr. Hawke you're here," the woman stated. "He and his son are having a...discussion right this minute."

"So I can hear," Jennifer responded as the screaming once more increased to an ear-shattering volume. "Where are they?"

"In the dining room."

"Could you show me where the dining room is?"

At first the woman appeared hesitant, but then she shrugged and led the way. Jennifer stood in the open doorway and gazed into the room. Trevor and Damien were completely oblivious to her presence. Trevor sat at the table with his hands clenched in his lap, his face a model of carefully controlled patience. Damien was screaming so loudly that Jennifer couldn't understand a word he was saying, but Trevor's responses were low and inaudible to her.

Jennifer grimaced when Damien suddenly grabbed what looked suspiciously like an antique Waterford crystal water glass and flung it at the wall, where it shattered into a thousand pieces. She was convinced it was antique Waterford crystal when she saw the look of horror on Trevor's face, and she took a step into the room, certain that at any moment he'd leap from his chair and strangle his son. But Trevor's hands merely clenched more tightly in his lap, and he murmured something she couldn't hear.

Evidently Damien had heard, and he once again began screaming. This time he threw a china bread plate at the wall. Jennifer closed her eyes and counted to ten as her temper began to stir. Then she turned and headed after the housekeeper. When Trevor had said "temper tantrums," he hadn't been kidding.

She walked through the swinging door at the end of the hall and entered the kitchen. The housekeeper glanced up in surprise, and Jennifer smiled.

"May I have a glass of water?"

"A glass of water?" the woman repeated. "Sure."

"Thank you." Jennifer accepted the glass and walked back toward the dining room.

Damien was still screaming, and Trevor was still murmuring. Neither of them saw her until she walked up behind Damien's wheelchair and dumped the glass of water over his head.

The screaming stopped abruptly, and Jennifer smiled, let out a relieved sigh and said, "Peace at last." She sat down on the chair next to Trevor and eyed his plate. "If I'd known you were having fresh shrimp for dinner, I'd have arrived sooner."

She stole a shrimp off his plate, dipped it into the cocktail sauce and popped it into her mouth. Trevor gulped as his eyes automatically glued themselves to her mouth, and it suddenly took all his willpower to keep from leaning over and licking off the dab of cocktail sauce that clung to her bottom lip. What was it about her that made her so appealing? he wondered desperately, finding himself envious of her tongue as it snaked out to lick the sauce away. He knew a hundred more beautiful women and a hundred more who fit in with his life-style. Jennifer Anne O'Brien Hamilton was a renegade, and the last thing he needed in his life was a renegade.

"Dad, she threw water on me!" Damien suddenly wailed.

Trevor blinked as if coming out of a trance and then stared at Jennifer accusingly. "You dumped water on Damien's head!"

Jennifer glanced from Trevor to Damien and back to Trevor. "Don't worry, Trevor. He's wash and wear. He won't shrink. Will you, Damien?" she questioned, glancing back at the boy.

Damien opened his mouth to respond, and Jennifer reached over and placed her fingers against his lips. "Angel would be very disappointed in you, Damien. You just broke some very beautiful, very expensive dishes. Where she comes from, her entire family probably could have eaten for a week on the cost of that glass alone. I think you owe your father an apology, don't you?"

She managed to swallow the chuckle that threatened as she tried to decide whether Trevor or Damien looked more dumbfounded at the suggestion of an apology. It was definitely Trevor, she decided when Damien shot Jennifer a confused look and very quietly said, "I'm sorry, Dad. I shouldn't have broken the dishes. I'll pay for them out of my allowance."

Trevor parted his lips to refuse the offer, but one glance at Jennifer's face told him he'd be in trouble if he did. "All right, Damien. I'll deduct the cost of the dishes from your allowance. If you're through eating, you may be excused. Dr. Hamilton and I have some business to discuss."

"Does that mean I don't get dessert?" Damien asked. He glanced guiltily toward Jennifer.

Trevor also glanced at her as if seeking approval. She smiled and asked, "What's for dessert? Maybe I'll join you."

"I don't know," Trevor answered. "Damien, why don't you go ask Mrs. Ferguson what we're having for dessert?"

"Okay," he agreed, and he maneuvered the wheelchair away from the table.

"Why did you dump a glass of water on him?" Trevor asked the moment he thought Damien was out of earshot. Then he realized he was really more interested in the way she was polishing off the remaining shrimp on his plate. Until now he'd never considered the act of eating sensuous, but it was definitely that when Jennifer Hamilton was the one doing the eating. She savored each morsel, chewing it carefully and then swallowing it with a heavenly sigh as her tongue flicked out to encircle her lips. He couldn't have controlled his body's response if he'd wanted to, and he really didn't want to, he realized, a smile touching his lips.

"He needed to cool down," Jennifer answered. "What was he shouting about, anyway?"

She arched a curious brow as she watched Trevor's cheeks flush a dull crimson, and he glanced away as if embarrassed. "I told him he had to spend the weekend at his grandparents' house."

"And that sent him into a rage?" Jennifer asked, incredulous. "Most kids love to see their grandparents."

"Damien normally enjoys seeing them, but…well, he found out that a, uh, friend was coming for the weekend, and…"

"Say no more," Jennifer said nonchalantly, trying to ignore the jealousy that ripped through her. She had no reason—or right, for that matter—to feel jealous.

She glanced toward him and wondered what his friend looked like. Probably sophisticated, polished and oh, so very proper. Everything she wasn't, she thought with an inward sigh. Oh, well. She didn't fit the sophisticated, polished and oh, so very proper mold, anyway. If her mother, Monica Fleming O'Brien Barrington, had never been able to pound her into it, no one could.

"You said on the phone that you had come up with a solution for Damien's treatment," Trevor stated, startling her out of her reverie. "Did you find him a counselor?"

"In a manner of speaking," Jennifer answered. She popped another shrimp into her mouth and shrugged. "I've decided to let Damien live at Hamilton House."

"That's wonderful!" Trevor exclaimed in delight. "Edward said that if you…"

His voice trailed off, and another embarrassed flush stained his cheeks as he realized what he'd almost revealed.

Jennifer laughed and shook her head in rueful amusement. "Don't be embarrassed, Trevor. I know exactly what Edward said. He knew that if I saw Damien, I'd have to take him in. We all have our weaknesses. Unfortunately Edward is quite aware of most of mine."

"Do you mind taking him in, Jennifer? I don't want to force him on you."

"Mind?" Jennifer repeated. She shook her head. "No, I don't mind. I'll just have to fit him into my schedule and hope for the best. Does Damien know you want him to live at Hamilton House?"

"No. I didn't discuss it with him because it wasn't a certainty. I couldn't see approaching the subject until it needed to be approached. When do you want him to move in?"

"Anytime you want. There's a general meeting at Hamilton House tonight, and I'll brief the kids on what's going on. We'll move a cot for him into my office, and we'll work something out so that he's not alone at night. Outside of that, there aren't many details to take care of. Whenever you're ready to move Damien into Hamilton House, we'll be ready for him."

"You lied to me!" Damien suddenly shrieked from the doorway. Startled, both Jennifer and Trevor turned in his direction. "You said you didn't want Sylvia to live here, but you do, and you're going to send me away to live in that crummy old place with all those crummy old people because you hate me!"

"Damien, that's not true!" Trevor exclaimed in alarm. "I love you. I'm not sending you away. I—"

"I hate you!" Damien interrupted, tears rolling down his cheeks. "I hate you, and I want my mama. I don't want Sylvia to live here. I want my mama!"

Jennifer's heart broke as she watched Damien bury his face in his hands and sob hysterically. She glanced toward Trevor, and her heart broke again. He looked so stricken. For a moment she couldn't decide which one to go to first, but Damien was the child. Trevor's comfort would have to wait until later. She rose from her chair and crossed quickly to the boy. She knelt in front of him and wrapped her arms around him. He buried his head against her chest and clung to her as if she were his lifeline.

"Cry it all out, sweetheart," she murmured as she brushed his still-damp hair back from his forehead and pressed a kiss against it. "Cry it all out."

"Damien," Trevor said quietly as he moved to join them.

Tentatively he laid his hand on his son's shoulder, but Damien flinched, "Don't touch me! I hate you!"

Jennifer glanced up at Trevor, and her eyes filled with tears at the totally beaten look that etched his face. He seemed to age ten years before her eyes as his shoulders drooped and he gave a weary shake of his head.

"Damien, I love you. Let me talk to you. Please," he pleaded.

"You don't love me," Damien sobbed, clinging desperately to Jennifer. "You hate me. You hate me because I . . ."

His voice trailed off as his sobs overwhelmed him. Tears began to roll down Jennifer's cheeks. He hadn't had to finish the sentence. She knew exactly what he was feeling. As far as he was concerned, his father had to hate him because he'd been responsible for his mother's death. She swallowed the moan that rose to her throat as an old wound was ripped open inside her. She wanted to keen as she rocked Damien back and forth, but she remained quiet and continued to hold him.

When his sobs began to subside, she kissed his forehead again, wiped at her own tear-stained cheeks and smiled when he finally looked up at her.

"Feeling better?" she inquired.

Damien shook his head and swiped childishly at his eyes. "Will you help me get into bed?"

"I'll help you, Damien," Trevor said eagerly.

Damien didn't say a word, but the glare he shot his father was more eloquent than any words he could have spoken. Trevor glanced helplessly at Jennifer, and she tried to give him a reassuring smile.

"I'll help you, Damien." She rose and moved behind the wheelchair.

As they left the silent room, Jennifer's heart ached for Trevor as much as it did for Damien.

The boy's room was on the first floor and had a connecting bath. Jennifer sat patiently in a chair by his window while she waited for him to prepare for bed.

When he finally came out of the bathroom, she asked. "Did you brush your teeth?"

He nodded and ducked his head shyly. "I can't put my pajama bottoms on by myself."

"Well, I think I can help," Jennifer said, accepting the bottoms he handed to her.

Her brow furrowed into a frown as she eyed his almost emaciated legs revealed beneath his white briefs.

Trevor was right. If Damien didn't get onto his feet soon, he'd be handicapped for the rest of his life. Once the pajamas were on, she helped him into bed and sat on the edge, brushing his hair back from his eyes.

"Damien, your father is not sending you away. He wants you to come live with me for a while because he thinks I can help you. You've been very sick, and sometimes when you've been very sick, you have to go to special places to help you get well."

"He hates me," he whispered, turning his head away from her. "He wants me to go away so Sylvia can live here."

"No," Jennifer disagreed, and caught his chin, forcing him to look at her. "Damien, if he wants her to live here, she'll live here with you. Your father loves you very much, and he'd never live with someone who didn't want you here."

"Then why does he always send me away when she comes?" he asked, his eyes filling with new tears. "He always sends me away. Why?"

"Because sometimes grown-up people need time alone, Damien. It's called courting, and when you get a little older, you'll understand."

"I don't want her living here, Jenny. I want my mama."

"I know," Jennifer consoled. She pressed a kiss to his forehead. "But your mama will always be here, Damien. In fact, she'll always be with you wherever you go, because she's right in your heart, and she'll never leave your heart."

"I miss her," he whispered, and turned his head away again.

"I know you do, but eventually that missing will go away. I promise."

"I hate him," he said then. "I don't like him anymore."

"Oh, Damien." She sighed, knowing that tonight was not the time to reason with him. He was just too young to understand that his father had to go on with his life. Once he was at Hamilton House, she'd work with him. With any luck, she'd be able to convince him that it was all right for Trevor to fall in love with another woman.

"Good night, Damien," she said, pulling the sheets up around his shoulders. "Have sweet dreams."

He didn't answer, and she knew he was pretending to be asleep. She'd pulled that same trick a thousand times herself. With another sigh, she rose from the edge of the bed and walked from his room. Now she'd have to try to comfort Trevor.

She found him in the living room, standing in front of the floor-to-ceiling windows that looked out over the gardens. He held a glass of Scotch that Jennifer suspected had been much fuller when he'd poured it.

"Did you get him into bed all right?" Trevor asked dully when she moved to his side.

"He's in bed."

"I'm sorry you had to witness that. Maybe I should have talked to him about living at Hamilton House."

"No, you shouldn't have," she immediately assured him. "Until you knew for certain, there was no need to broach the subject. He's hurting, Trevor, and you're the person he's striking out at because he loves you and you're convenient."

"I know," he said wearily, "but knowing doesn't make it any easier. He's my world, Jennifer. When he says he hates me, it's as if he's put a knife right through my heart."

"He doesn't hate you, Trevor."

Trevor shrugged and gulped down a healthy portion of Scotch. He shivered. "I'm so cold, Jennifer. I feel like I'm freezing."

Automatically she slid her arm around his waist, and his arm came around her shoulders, clutching her with the same desperation that Damien's arms had. Jennifer wanted to pull his head down to her chest, brush his hair back from his forehead and tell him to cry it all out. Instead she leaned her head against his shoulder and ran her hand up and down his side in a soothing gesture.

"It's not going to work now, you know," he said with a defeated sigh. "If I send him to Hamilton House, he'll be convinced that I want him out of the way."

"Why do you always send him away when your... friend comes?" she asked.

Trevor let out a mirthless laugh. "When I first started dating Sylvia, Damien went crazy. I told Edward I was going to stop dating her, and he gave me hell. He said that Damien had to learn to accept that his mother was gone and that I was still here. He had to see that life goes on." He shrugged and took another swallow of Scotch.

"I didn't like it, but I continued to see Sylvia. But whenever I'd bring her to the house, Damien would be so... impossible that tonight's little scene in the dining room seemed like a Sunday picnic. Since she lives out of town, I decided that when I invited her down, I'd just send him to stay with my parents. It worked well until tonight, when he overheard me talking to Sylvia on the telephone. He got it into his head that

I'm trying to get rid of him, and nothing I said would make him believe otherwise.''

Jennifer nodded and took hold of his hand. She brought his drink to her lips and took a sip, unaware of the flame that leaped in his eyes. When she released his hand, he turned the glass and brought it to his lips, his tongue touching the rim where her lips had been. He wanted her, he realized, and his hand began to tremble. He wanted her more than he'd ever wanted any other woman. But why her?

"Damien's feeling threatened," she stated, and she glanced up at Trevor with a consoling smile. "He can't help that. He adored his mother, and he adores you. He lost her, and now he's afraid he's going to lose you."

"So what do you suggest? Do I become a hermit?"

There was a touch of dry humor in his tone, and Jennifer's hazel eyes brightened with laughter, becoming gleaming shards of sea green that matched her simple cotton sundress. Trevor stared down into those eyes, completely mesmerized. She felt so right tucked beneath his arm, her hip resting against his hip, her thigh against his thigh and her arm around his waist. It took every ounce of his control to keep from crushing her to him. He wanted to feel every soft curve of her body nestled against his harder lines. He wanted to lose himself in her.

"I don't think you need to do anything quite so drastic," she said with a teasing laugh that denied the desire stirring inside. She could feel his tension and automatically responded to it. He wanted her. She wanted him. The question was, what were they going to do about it? If they were smart, nothing.

"You're sure?"

"I'm sure."

"So where do I go from here, Jennifer? If I send him to you, he's going to be certain I don't want him, but if I keep him here..." His voice trailed off, and he heaved a meaningful sigh.

Jennifer gazed out the window thoughtfully. "There may be a way to convince him that he has nothing to fear from your relationship with Sylvia."

"How?"

"You could also live at Hamilton House."

"Me?"

"Why not?" she questioned, raising her eyes to his face. "You'd have to share a room with a couple of the boys, but we could fit you in. Then Damien would know you weren't deserting him. He wouldn't feel threatened, and it would certainly make it easier for me to help him if he didn't."

"I suppose I could sleep downstairs with him."

"No!" Jennifer immediately exclaimed. Taking note of his confused expression, she explained, "I want you separated from him, at least, a little. He's too dependent on you as it is. Having you in the house will be enough. Are you willing?"

He drew in a deep breath and then let it out slowly. "There's only one problem with that solution."

"What's that?"

"I want you."

Jennifer blinked at the blunt voicing of her own thoughts of only moments before, and she glanced away so he wouldn't see her blush. It wasn't embarrassment, but a feminine response to his words that ran so deep it hurt.

"We're both adults. I think we could handle it."

"We could. The problem is, I don't want to."

"What about your . . . friend?"

"That's all she is. A friend. I care about Sylvia, but neither of us has ever felt that our relationship would develop into something permanent."

"We have nothing in common, Trevor."

"Opposites attract."

Jennifer shook her head and stepped forward to lean her forehead against the cool glass of the window. Trevor had said he felt as if he were freezing. She felt as if she were burning up, and it was a disturbing sensation. After taking a few slow, deep breaths in an effort to control her racing heart, she glanced up at him with a thoughtful frown.

"Trevor, I was also married, and my husband was killed in a plane accident a few years ago. My marriage was fairy-tale romantic. We shared everything. Tom would be a hard act to follow. It's one reason I've never become involved with another man."

"Never?" Trevor questioned, and found himself oddly pleased with her confession.

"Never."

"Jennifer, if I move into Hamilton House with Damien, I'll be moving in wanting you. I'm a strong enough man to take no for an answer, but I'm not a strong enough man not to try. If you agree to take Damien on, then you agree to take me on at the same time. God only knows what this attraction is between us, but you feel it, too, don't you?" he finished hesitantly.

"Yes," she admitted. "I feel it, too. But just what are you proposing here? A one-night stand? A momentary fling? An affair?"

"I don't really know what I'm proposing, Jennifer. I'm not a man who engages in one-night stands or flings, so I guess I must be proposing an . . . affair."

"I see," she responded quietly. "Just what are the rules of this affair? Do we enter into it with our eyes wide open and no strings attached? This is all for a little fun and nothing more?"

Trevor frowned as he watched her shift from one foot to the other and lace and unlace her fingers in agitation. He definitely wasn't handling this well. The problem was, he didn't have the answers to her questions.

He decided to take the easy way out. "Haven't you ever heard of seizing the moment?"

"Yes, and it's always sounded like Russian roulette to me. A very wise man once told me that two people can't enter into an affair without one of them getting hurt. No matter how much you say there are no strings attached, someone is bound to fall in love."

"That sounds like something Edward would say."

"It does sound like Edward," she responded with a brittle laugh, "but actually, it was my husband, Tom. I was reluctant to become involved with him, and yet I was drawn to him. I wanted to take the easy way out. No commitments. He was right. I fell in love with him, and luckily for me, he fell in love with me."

Trevor stepped forward, caught her chin and turned her face toward him. "I'm willing to take the risk, Jennifer."

"What risk? Falling in love? An impossible love?"

"Why would it be impossible?"

"Because in less than a year the current Hamilton House will become a temporary refuge for runaways, and my permanent location will be a new Hamilton

House in the country. More than a hundred miles from here. I've already bought the land and begun construction. It's a dream that I've had since . . . well, for years," she said, unwilling to admit her past to him. "If we did fall in love, would you be willing to give up your practice and move to the country?"

He shook his head. "No. I've worked too long and too hard to build it. It isn't just a practice to me it's . . ."

"What you are?" Jennifer offered when his voice trailed off as he searched for an appropriate descriptive term.

"Yes. It's what I am," he answered with a smile.

"And that's what Hamilton House is to me, Trevor. It's what I am. I could never walk away from it. Never. Not even for love."

"And if I swore I'd never ask you to?"

"That could also prove to be an impossibility."

"Not if I swear."

His head was lowering toward her, and Jennifer had neither the inclination nor the strength to pull away from him. She wanted him to kiss her, she admitted. She wanted him to make love to her. But why him? Why was she so drawn to him?

His lips were only a breath away when he murmured, "I've been daydreaming about kissing you since I first saw you this afternoon."

"You have?"

"Uh-huh. What about you?"

"Just kiss me, Trevor."

"And then?"

"And then tell me you're moving into Hamilton House."

"I wasn't kidding, Jennifer. If I move in, you're agreeing to take me on."

"I know you weren't kidding."

"You're sure, then?"

"I'm sure."

"What about your Russian roulette?"

"I've always lived dangerously."

"Oh, Jenny," he whispered, and he moved in so close that even a cat's whisker couldn't have slipped between them. She tilted her head up, parting her lips slightly in anticipation.

"Oh, my," he said, catching her waist and drawing her against him. All the breath rushed from her lungs as her breasts were crushed against his chest. Her arms rose to wrap around his neck, and her lips parted even more. His head began to lower.

"Dr. Hawke?" Mrs. Ferguson called out, and Trevor and Jennifer leaped away from each other like two errant children.

"What is it, Mrs. Ferguson?" he called back.

"Damien's asking for you. It sounds urgent."

"I'm coming," Trevor answered. He gazed at Jennifer in resignation. "Later?" he questioned.

"Later," she answered.

"I'm disappointed."

Her lips curved up in a wry smile. "Me, too."

"At Hamilton House?"

"At Hamilton House."

"Maneuvering around Damien and twenty teenagers will be quite a chore."

"Wait until you meet my assistant. You don't have any idea what a chore it will be."

He raised his fingers to her lips and traced the contours of her mouth. "I'd climb Mount Everest to kiss you."

"I don't think it will be *that* hard."

"I have to go. Damien's calling."

"I know."

"Are you absolutely, positively certain about this, Jennifer?" he questioned uncertainly.

"No, but I'm willing to give it chance and see what will happen."

He smiled, pressed his fingers to her lips and walked from the room, leaving her staring after him in bemusement.

"Why him?" she asked aloud as she walked into the foyer and retrieved her purse. "Why him?" she repeated moments later when she climbed into her car and began backing it, grimacing at the unsightly oil stain the Chevy had deposited on his immaculate Beverly Hills driveway.

Chapter Three

Jennifer's husband, Tom, had always said that a good game of darts helped put things into perspective. Jennifer smiled in fond memory as she flung darts at the dart board. She still missed him. Missed his bright red hair, bright green eyes and his thousands of freckles that she'd never been able to get a firm count on, no matter how hard she'd tried. She missed his sunny smile and his dry humor, but she no longer felt that aching pain of loss when she thought of him.

"Come on, I want a bull's-eye," she muttered in true Thomas Hamilton fashion before flinging her last dart. It wasn't a bull's-eye but close enough for her limited talents. She gathered the darts and moved back to the center of the empty community room to start over.

As she began to throw the darts again, she dismissed Tom from her thoughts and let her mind mull over the events of the day. Trevor and Damien Hawke had burst into her life and tossed her entire world upside down. Trevor had resurrected feelings of passion so long dormant that she'd forgotten they existed. Damien had ripped open an old wound and touched her heart in a way it hadn't been touched in years. She couldn't have walked away from either of them if she'd tried, and Edward had known it.

Her head instantly pivoted when she heard a sound behind her, and she smiled fondly when her assistant, Theresa Baker, ambled into the room. Theresa's short cap of dark unruly curls tumbled in disorder around her pleasant, round face. Her dark brown eyes drooped from weariness, and she let out a sigh of relief when she let her plump body collapse onto the worn sofa.

"What a day." She yawned, not even wasting the energy to cover her mouth.

"You can say that again." Jennifer tossed another dart. "Bed check over?"

"Racer and Angel report that all heads are accounted for. Having them as president and vice president of Hamilton House has been a joy. I don't think we've ever had anyone as good since I've been here."

"I think they're the best we've ever had," Jennifer agreed.

When she and Tom had opened Hamilton House, they'd had the kids elect a president and a vice president. Then they'd turned the entire operation over to the kids. They were required to budget the funds and pay the bills for everything from food to utilities and clothing to medical expenses. They worked in teams and performed all the chores from cleaning the building to preparing meals. The most useful lesson learned at Hamilton House was basic survival. The most important lesson learned was that all people were treated with love, friendship, understanding, trust and respect. In Jennifer's book, those were the five basic ingredients to any successful relationship, be it friendship or more.

"I'm always surprised at how these kids take everything in stride," Theresa commented thoughtfully. "I expected at least a couple of protests when you announced that Dr. Hawke and his son were moving in and that you wanted them to help keep an eye on Damien."

"So did I."

"Did you see how Angel lit up like a Christmas tree?"

Jennifer nodded. "Yes, and I was very pleased that she volunteered to stay down on this floor with Damien. Evidently they've already formed a bond. I think she can help him, and I'm certain he'll help her."

"I wish we could convince her to go back home," Theresa said.

"We may in time. It's difficult to convince someone who's casting herself into the role of a martyr that she's wrong. She really believes that her staying away will allow her family enough extra money to help her sister. The problem is, no matter how much money they have, her sister will never be out of a wheelchair. Angel knows that and has pretty much accepted it, but she still wants to have hope."

"If Damien does recover, couldn't that give her more false hope?"

"Not if I handle it right," Jennifer answered with a sigh. "I'm hoping that with Angel's help he will recover, and that knowing that she helped him recover will help her accept her sister's fate. She can't help her, but she did help someone else. She did her part, so to speak."

"You're amazing, Jennifer. How do you crawl inside people like that?"

"I don't know. I suppose it's a gift."

"A rare gift, but, then, you're a rare lady. Why are you playing darts?"

"I'm trying to solve a problem."

"What problem?"

"His name is Dr. Trevor Hawke."

Theresa let out a low whistle. "Do I hear the stirrings of chickens and frogs?"

Jennifer laughed and missed the dart board completely. "They're that loud, huh?"

"I thought you delivered that speech a little more vehemently tonight than you normally do. Trying to convince yourself?"

"Yep."

"Why?"

"Why?"

"We have the oddest echo in this room."

"Bad acoustics."

"Does he feel the same way?"

"He says he does."

"Wow. Things will get steamy around here. Fleet of foot, too. Do you have any idea how hard it is to avoid twenty kids?"

"It's avoiding you I'm worried about."

"I'm a coconspirator. If I can't have a love life of my own, I'll live one vicariously."

"That's sick, Theresa."

"I think it's called voyeurism, Jennifer."

"Even worse."

"Are you really going to try to resist him? I heard it on the grapevine that he's a hunk."

"I thought the word *hunk* was out of date."

"Not in my vocabulary. Are you going to try to resist him?" Theresa repeated, plainly curious.

"I don't know," Jennifer answered. She grinned when the dart she tossed hit a bull's-eye. "Maybe I'll go after him with both barrels. I'd probably end up regretting it, but it might be fun."

"I'm all for that," Theresa said, and then she yawned again. "I'll see you in the morning."

Trevor stood at the window in Damien's room and stared out into the darkness. It had taken hours to get his son to sleep, and Trevor thought he'd never convince him that he wasn't sending him away. Damien still didn't believe that his father would be going to Hamilton House with him, but he would. On Monday morning.

Sylvia wouldn't be coming down for the weekend. He'd call her and cancel. But as far as Damien was concerned, he'd let him believe that the weekend plans were remaining the same.

Edward was right, Trevor admitted. Damien had to understand that his father was still alive and had to go on with his life. If he gave in to his demands now, Damien might interfere with his plans for Jennifer. Damn. What was it about her that was so intriguing? he wondered yet again. Why was he so drawn to her?

He raised his eyes to the sky and watched a cloud drift across the moon. In slow motion his life began to move through his mind, and he wondered when he'd last been really happy. Several events were significant, special—graduating from medical school, opening his practice, marrying. Of course, the most significant and moving moment was Damien's birth.

But he couldn't clearly define a time when he'd been happy for more than a fleeting moment. Being raised as Reginald Hawke's only son had been more a burden than a blessing. The internationally famed entrepreneur was a hard man, and he'd been furious when Trevor announced his plans to become a doctor instead of taking over the conglomerate holdings of Hawke International. His mother had, as always, stepped in and soothed the ruffled feathers until the two men had been able to sit down and really talk. His father hadn't liked it but had finally resigned himself to "his son, the doctor" instead of "his son, the entrepreneur."

Patricia had been equally disappointed in him, and as much as he hated to admit it, it hadn't been too long after they'd married that both had discovered that they'd been "in like" with each other and not "in love." Their marriage probably wouldn't have lasted a year if Damien hadn't been conceived on their honeymoon. Patricia had adored her son as much as Trevor did, and they'd agreed to stay together for his sake.

The memory of that decision brought tears to Trevor's eyes. Poor Patricia had spent most of her adult life trapped in a marriage that hadn't necessarily made her unhappy, but that had certainly never made her really happy. He felt guilty about that. She should have had more, had the experiences that would have made her happy. He'd give almost anything if he could remember ever seeing a completely joyous, uninhibited smile on her face like the smile on Jennifer's this morning when she opened the closet door and those two boys fell out.

Suddenly Trevor blinked as he realized that that was part of what was drawing him to her. Jennifer was happy. There was no artifice or guile to her. There were no emotional masks in place. She was simply Jennifer, and when you were around her, you instinctively knew you could be you and she would accept that.

He also realized that he was actually looking forward to moving into Hamilton House. He wouldn't need all those masks that he kept safely tucked away in his little black bag to bring out for each specific occasion. He wouldn't have to be anyone but Trevor. A wry smile touched his lips. Here he was, almost thirty-eight years old, and it sounded as if he were going through an identity crisis. And maybe he was. Since Patricia's death he'd been filled with more questions than answers. He had a feeling that if anyone could help him find some of the answers, it was Jennifer.

He turned away from the window and crossed to his son's bed. He gazed down into Damien's peacefully sleeping face and tenderly brushed the hair off his forehead.

"I love you," he whispered and then bent to kiss the top of his head. "You're my world, and you always will be." With those words spoken, he left the room.

Jennifer's Monday morning began at the crack of dawn. She was up, dressed and on her way to the new Hamilton House site before the rest of the house had stirred.

She spent most of the day with the architect and the contractor, and they argued and compromised and argued some more before they finally resolved their problems. After the meeting, she wandered to the clearing that she'd christened Love's Magic Meadow and collapsed on its thick carpet of grass to enjoy its peaceful solitude.

Only she knew the significance this parcel of land held for her. She'd never even haggled over the price when she'd discovered it was up for sale. She'd offered what the owner was asking and had smiled when she'd looked into his face, knowing he'd wondered if he'd asked too little. Actually, she would have paid much more, because this meadow had been her salvation.

She'd been fourteen when she ran away from home. Three days later, terrified and lonely, she'd stumbled into the meadow. From the moment she'd entered it, all her fear had fled.

She tipped her head back now and gazed up into the verdant foliage overhead. Birds sang and crickets chirped. There was a colorful profusion of wild flowers, and she gently, reverently, caressed the petals of the single orange flower that seemed to bloom here eternally. It was that orange flower that had allowed her to survive her two-year hiatus as a runaway. It had planted a special message in her heart, a message that she'd carried with her and passed on to every person she met. It was a message to be shared because that message was, love could make it better.

The meadow had always been essential in her counseling, and soon it would no longer be a fantasy image that she projected to her kids, but a vital reality. They'd be able to sit in the meadow and absorb its healing powers on their own, just as she had so many years before. This precious spot was a little bit of Eden that God hadn't stolen away.

The sun had nearly set when she reluctantly rose to her feet and made her way back to the construction site. It was a good two-hour drive back to Hamilton House. Trevor and Damien would have arrived by now, and a new chapter in her life was ready to begin.

When Jennifer walked through the door of Hamilton House, she was greeted by the sounds of laughter emanating from the community room. She leaned against the wall outside the door, and her lips curved into a grin as she listened to the chatter within. She ought to strangle the little devils, she thought with an inward chuckle. Finally she'd heard enough and pushed herself away from the wall. It was time to rescue Trevor.

She nonchalantly strolled into the room, her hands stuffed into the pockets of her shorts. Cheerfully, she said, "Good evening, everyone."

Immediately five teenagers ducked their heads guiltily. Trevor stared at her with a confused, lost expression, and Damien glanced up from a game of checkers he was playing with Angel and said, "Hi, Jenny. You missed supper."

"I sure did, Damien," she agreed, her eyes straying to the five teenagers who were busily looking everywhere in the room but at her. "I heard," she announced ominously, and dropped down onto the arm of the overstuffed chair Trevor sat in. Five young faces flushed crimson. "You know the rules, kids. What kind of game were you playing?"

"We weren't playing a game," Stretch grumbled, scowling at the worn toe of his running shoe. "We were just talking."

"But in what language?" Jennifer asked. She glanced toward Trevor with a consoling smile. His lips tilted tentatively upward in response, making him look so vulnerable that Jennifer's pulse picked up speed. Her cheeks reddened, and she resisted the urge to fan her face. He was a potent elixir, and if someone ever managed to bottle him, women all over the world would be in trouble.

"Kid talk," Licorice replied to her question, the familiar piece of red licorice dangling from his mouth.

"Kid talk," Jennifer repeated, giving a disappointed shake of her head. "The first rule you learn at Hamilton House is that the kid talk stays out on the sidewalk. Inside we speak English."

"We were speaking English." Sundance tilted her small chin in a show of defiance.

"But you were not *communicating* English," Jennifer admonished, her gaze shifting from one teenager to another until they squirmed uneasily in their seats. "As punishment, I expect all of you to interpret what I'm going to say and explain it to me in the morning. I hope you're ready, because I'm only going to say this once. Here goes."

She drew in a deep breath and said, "There are dramatic vicissitudes of the English language in every generation that obfuscate communication. Interlocution becomes a labyrinth that assiduously eliminates the mature."

"Huh?" five pubescent voices gasped.

Jennifer gave them a smug grin and announced, "That, kids, is the English language. I suggest you look it up in your lexicon." She shifted her attention to Trevor. "Trevor, would you like to join me?"

"Sure." His lips twitched, and he fought to control a grin as he rose to his feet, gallantly taking her hand to ease her off the arm of the chair.

Jennifer cast a disapproving stare at the kids, then winked at Trevor and led him out of the room. As soon as they were out of sight of the door, she placed her hand on his arm to halt his progress and barely controlled the giggle that surfaced when one of the kids asked, "What in heck is a lexicon?"

"How would I know?" another grumbled. "I guess we'd better look it up in the dictionary."

"I'll get it," one volunteered, sighing heavily. "Whatever happened to old-fashioned punishment like screaming and grounding? I'd rather have a lecture than Jenny's punishments any day."

"Yeah, but we knew we were wrong," another admitted. "We also knew if she caught us, we'd be in trouble."

"Does anyone know how to spell 'lexicon'?"

"You were a little rough on them, weren't you?" Trevor whispered when Jennifer once again began leading him down the hallway.

"No rougher than they were on you," she answered. She opened a closet door, glanced covertly up and down the hallway and, finding it clear, grabbed his arm and pulled him into the closet with her.

"Jennifer, why are we in the closet?" Trevor whispered when she closed the door, enveloping them in darkness.

"Can you see me?" she asked with a muffled giggle.

"No. It's dark in here."

"I know."

"So why are we in the closet?" he questioned again, his voice threaded with amusement.

"There aren't any kids in here," she explained.

"That's true," he answered. "Just mating dice. But that doesn't tell me why we're in the closet."

"We're in here because of chickens and frogs, Trevor."

"Chickens and frogs? I hate to say this, Jennifer, but I think I was better off with the kids. What in the world are you talking about?"

"That, Dr. Hawke," she purred, "is Dr. Jennifer Hamilton's version of the birds and the bees. You owe me a kiss. I'm here to collect."

Trevor nearly trembled in anticipation, and he drew a deep breath and leaned back against the wall.

"You are, huh?"

"Sure enough," she whispered, and reached out blindly to encounter the breadth of his chest. Nice, she decided as her fingers stroked the blue knit fabric that clung to a tantalizing mass of muscle. Very nice. "Are you going to kiss me, or should I turn on the light and pull out a deck of cards? By the way, how good are you at poker?"

"I'm a lousy poker player," he answered. He curled his hand around her wrist and tugged lightly, pulling her against him. His lips moved across her temple in a butterfly caress.

"Are you really lousy at poker?" she asked breathlessly as his arms wrapped around her waist and his large hands molded her body to every hard, delicious line of his own.

"Abominable," he assured her, and sighed when she arched her head back so he could slide his lips down the swanlike length of her neck.

"Then don't play cards with the kids," she warned, and slid her hands wantonly up his shoulders, then entwined her arms around his neck. "If you do, you'll lose your home, your car and most likely your practice. I'm afraid they cheat."

"You sure do feel good, lady," he told her as his lips stole a quick kiss and his hands explored the soft swell of her hips. "They cheat, huh?"

"Afraid so."

His lips captured hers in a gentle, persuasive assault, and she gave a low moan and burrowed more closely against him. Her fingers buried themselves in the rich depths of his mink-brown hair, and he groaned urgently when her lips parted in invitation. Time seemed suspended until he released her from the kiss and leaned his head back against the wall, struggling to control his erratic breathing and the frantic rise and fall of his chest. No amount of daydreaming could have prepared him for this! She was pure ambrosia.

Jennifer rested her head against his chest and listened to his heart pound in time with her own. It had been such a long time since she'd been held in a man's arms, and she remained very still, luxuriating in the sensation.

When his heart had slowed and his breathing had calmed, she asked, "So how was the kiss?"

"Fishing for compliments?" he teased.

"Of course."

He laughed as he anchored her hips to him with one hand and raised the other to stroke the outer curve of her breast. She trembled in response, and he smiled tenderly.

"The kiss was more wonderful than I'd hoped for," he answered honestly. "Whatever is sparking between us is special, Jenny, though I can't help but wonder why. We are definitely a mismatched couple."

"You can say that again." She sighed and rubbed her cheek against his shirt. "But whatever that special something is, Trevor, it's too potent and it's moving too fast. We're going to have to exercise some control, give ourselves some time."

"Is that your way of telling me I'm going to have to make reservations for a quick kiss in the closet?"

"Yes. Do you mind?"

"Mind?" he repeated, and rubbed his chin against her hair. "Yes, sweet Jenny, I mind, but I'll survive." Then he chuckled and asked, "By the way, just what did all that mumbo jumbo mean that you told the kids a few minutes ago?"

"Look it up in your lexicon, Dr. Hawke." She giggled, pressed a swift kiss to his lips and eased from his embrace. "Sleep well. I'll see you tomorrow."

"You're a damn tease," he grumbled good-naturedly as he watched her exit the closet.

Jennifer's hand snaked from beneath the sheet and fumbled for the wailing instrument beside her head. Groggily she brought the telephone receiver to her ear and yawned, "Yeah?" It was Trevor's answering service, and she told the woman she'd have Trevor return the call immediately.

With another yawn, she struggled into a sitting position and punched the top of her alarm clock to light the dial. While groaning at the early-morning hour, she shrugged into a short terry-cloth robe before making her way to the room Trevor was sharing with Racer and Long John.

A doctor's day was never done, she thought ruefully. She had her share of middle-of-the-night and early-morning emergencies, but she knew they were infrequent compared to Trevor's hectic schedule. She could only imagine that one good, uninterrupted night's sleep must seem like heaven to him.

Easing open the door, she stealthily crept to the edge of Trevor's bed and gazed down into the handsome face revealed in the silvery light of a moonbeam. His dark hair was tousled, giving him a rakish appearance. Those long, spiky lashes curled over high cheekbones. His strong chin showed a shading of beard, and his lips were curved into a soft smile, as if he were enjoying a pleasant dream. She hated to disturb him. In fact, what she'd really like to do, she thought dreamily, was pull back the sheet and climb in beside him.

Shame on you, Jennifer Anne Hamilton, she inwardly scolded, and with a recriminating shake of her head, she placed her hand on his shoulder, whispering, "Trevor?"

She let out a startled gasp when he immediately bolted upright in bed, causing her hand to slide down his bare chest. Years of conditioning must have trained him to wake instantly.

His fingers curled around her wrist before she could jerk her hand away, and he began to rub it in an unconsciously erotic motion up and down the smooth surface of his skin.

Her gaze settled on the wide expanse of sun-bronzed muscle and sinew that was bare to the waist, and the white line revealed just above the sheet indicated he wore nothing more than percale. It seemed strange to her that a man who exuded such virility wouldn't have hair on his chest. He was the most exciting specimen of masculinity she'd ever seen.

"Hi," he whispered huskily. "I sure hope this midnight rendezvous is for pleasure."

Jennifer glanced surreptitiously toward the sleeping figures in the other two beds. "Sorry, but it's business. Your service called."

"Oh, well, a man can always hope." He sighed, his eyes bright with humor. Then he tugged on her hand until he'd pulled her close enough for him to capture her lips in a quick kiss. "I'm sorry they woke you, sweetheart, but I'm afraid that's one of the hazards of the profession."

"I don't mind," she assured him. "The woman said that a patient of yours is at the emergency room. Do you think you'll have enough time for a cup of coffee before you leave?"

"Probably." He yawned and then pressed another quick kiss to her lips. "I'll call the service and meet you in the kitchen."

"Okay," she said, gazing at him with longing.

He growled deep in his throat and playfully swatted her bottom. "Remove yourself from this room, Jennifer, before I pull you into this bed and give these two young men a very visual lesson on mating."

"Chickens and frogs," she whispered impishly. He chuckled and gave an amused shake of his head.

Jennifer hummed a popular tune as she spread cream cheese over a freshly toasted bagel, unaware that Trevor stood in the doorway studying her. His gaze roved hungrily over her lush form before roaming around the kitchen. Hamilton House had turned out to be as big a surprise as its director.

He'd been amazed by the beautifully renovated warehouse, although the fact that it sat on the edge of an extremely rough neighborhood disturbed him. He didn't like the idea of Jennifer strolling along these streets. But she had done miraculous things to the old building, he acknowledged admiringly.

All the rooms were large and airy, and although the furniture was old and battered, there was an inviting, homey warmth wherever you went. He could see Jennifer's personality displayed in the cheerful colors that filled the house. In the kitchen, yellow-and-white-checkered curtains hung at the windows. There were two massive round oak tables that, according to Theresa, Jennifer had picked up for a ''steal'' and refinished herself. The kitchen counters were spacious, and he'd watched in amazement the night before as a group of laughing kids had worked together in military precision to prepare an astonishingly good meal.

''You look awfully domestic,'' he said as he strolled into the kitchen, and he sucked in a deep breath when Jennifer pivoted her head and smiled at him. This morning, her hazel eyes glinted like twinkling stars beneath the overhead light.

Her gaze moved over him with interest, and her smile widened.

''And you must be the best quick-change artist in the country,'' she announced after taking in his crisply pressed slacks, white shirt, blue silk tie and his smoothly shaven jaw. ''It has to be sinful to smell so good this time of morning,'' she teased as she gave a

delicate sniff of the air and tilted her head provocatively to the side.

"I am going to have to paint you," Trevor said with
a sigh as he twisted a lock of copper hair around his
finger and gave it a gentle tug.

"Are you an artist?" Jennifer inquired.

"I dabble at it. It helps me relax."

Her eyes widened as she recalled the emotionally
stirring paintings in his foyer, and she asked, "Are you
T?"

He looked surprised. "Uh-huh."

"Trevor, you're very good! Have you sold anything?"

"No. It's just a hobby."

"It's a gift, Trevor, and it's the kind of gift that
ought to be shared. You really should show your
work."

"Maybe someday," he said, flushing slightly at her
compliment.

Her lips curved up in an impish grin. "So, what
color are you going to paint me?"

"What color?" he repeated in confusion.

"What color?" she repeated playfully as she handed
him half the bagel and a cup of coffee. "I think my
arms should be blue, but my legs? Hmm, I don't
know. You're the artist. What do you think?"

Trevor's eyes slid down to her long legs revealed
beneath the mid-thigh hem of her robe. He liked the
fact that she wasn't self-conscious about her body.
That was generally an indication of a good, healthy
attitude toward sex. The thought caused an uncomfortable burst of desire, and he shifted his stance to a
less revealing position, shook his head and said,
"Gorgeous. Definitely gorgeous."

"Is gorgeous a color?"

"No, gorgeous is definitely not a color." He set his coffee and bagel on the counter, leaned against it and wrapped an arm around her waist. As he pulled her between his rock-hard thighs, he said in his best professorial tone, "Gorgeous is a description, and you never paint over gorgeous."

"You don't?"

"You don't." He dropped a kiss on the end of her nose before instructing, "All you do with gorgeous is capture it on canvas for posterity. But first you must admire it."

"Is that what you're doing now?" she inquired breathlessly when his hands began to slide sensuously up and down her rib cage, his thumbs brushing in feathery strokes against the outer curves of her breasts.

"That's what I'm doing. Before an artist can put one stroke of gorgeous down on canvas, he must know his subject intimately."

"Trevor?" she whispered tremulously when he lowered his head and began to nibble along the side of her neck.

"Hmm?"

"What about your patient?"

"She's a hypochondriac. Probably nothing more than heartburn."

"Heartburn at this time of the morning?" Jennifer yelped when his lips strayed to the open neck of her robe, sending shock tremors through her so powerful she suspected they'd register on the Richter scale.

"She probably visited her favorite Mexican restaurant last night," he explained before letting out a wolf whistle as he released the belt on her robe and parted it. "Damn, Jennifer, you add a new dimension to the word *gorgeous*!"

She flushed deeply beneath his hot gaze as he surveyed the nearly diaphanous shorty pajamas. "I could come to the conclusion that you only want me for my body," she grumbled half-heartedly.

"You could," he agreed with a wicked grin. He raised his hand and brushed it across her breast, making her gasp as her nipple immediately became a turgid peak. "But you'd be wrong," he continued so conversationally that she wondered if this intimate play was even affecting him. "You are quite a woman, Dr. Jennifer Hamilton. Both brilliant and beautiful. I want to make love to you, Jenny."

The tautness of his smile told her that the intimate play had affected him just as volatilely as it had her.

"I know you do," she whispered hoarsely.

"And you want to make love to me," he stated knowingly.

"I do," she admitted artlessly.

"But you're going to make us wait." He sighed, closing her robe and rebelting it.

"I am," she affirmed.

"I understand," he stated in resignation.

"Do you?" she questioned.

He gave her a lopsided, boyish grin. "Not really."

"You'd better finish your coffee and bagel," she announced shakily when he settled his hands at her waist and drew her into firm contact with him.

"I'm not hungry," he muttered, "and caffeine this time of the morning plays hell on the nerves." He lightly kissed her lips and mumbled, "I can't believe you taste this good."

Her eyes closed in pure bliss. Her breasts were pressed lovingly against the wall of his chest, and his desire was intimately nestled into the cradle of her womanhood.

"Chickens and frogs," she whispered on a throaty sigh.

"We are definitely going to have to introduce your chickens and frogs to my birds and bees," he growled, and he captured her lips in a heart-stopping kiss.

It was like riding a roller coaster, she decided as his kiss began to deepen. You moved slowly upward, anticipation and suspense building as you waited for the inevitable approach to the crest, knowing you'd be plunging down the other side.

Her lips parted beneath the insistent pressure of his tongue, and her senses seemed to implode, spiraling inward to the hidden regions of her womb. Her arms wound eagerly around his neck, and her tongue began to duel passionately with his, challenging him, defying him to stop.

Trevor groaned and jerked his head away from the kiss. "Dear God, Jenny." He breathed harshly and rested his forehead against hers. "You make me want to crawl right inside you and become you. You are both a delight and a curse, Dr. Hamilton," he concluded wryly, "and I'd better get out of here while I can still move with a modicum of comfort."

He pressed a lingering kiss to the tip of her nose. "I'll see you this evening, sweetheart."

Jennifer nodded, her vocal chords paralyzed. She was still too stunned by the potency of their kiss. Her hand rose to feather across his cheek and along his jaw, pausing to let her index finger dip into the small cleft in the center of his chin. He caught her hand and lifted it to his lips, where he gently nipped each fingertip. It was unbearably erotic.

Dark violet eyes glowed like brilliant jewels through that spiky forest of lashes. She reached up to brush the errant strands of hair from his forehead, and he shook his head and smiled regretfully.

"I'd like nothing better than to stay here with you, sweetheart, but I do have a patient waiting. Maybe this evening we can pick up where we left off."

Reluctantly he eased Jennifer away from him, dropped a brief but totally devastating kiss onto her lips and walked out of the kitchen. It was a very long time before her brain could convince her legs that they could still walk.

Chapter Four

Jennifer's first encounter with the recalcitrant Damien occurred approximately four hours later. She was in her office, reviewing the month's budget the kids had prepared, when Theresa stuck her head into the office.

"Jenny, we have a problem."

"A problem?" Jennifer repeated, glancing up absently from the papers in front of her. "What kind of problem?"

"Damien refuses to go to school."

"I see." Jennifer laid her pencil down on top of the papers and rose. "I'll take care of him."

Damien was sitting in the community room with his arms folded mutinously over his chest. "I am not going to school," he enunciated carefully the moment Jennifer walked into the room.

"You *are* going to school," she enunciated just as carefully. "Everyone at Hamilton House goes to school, Damien. There are no exceptions."

"I don't have to go to school."

"You want to grow up to be a dummy?"

His glare was condescending. "I don't *have* to go to school. My dad hires someone to teach me."

"He doesn't at Hamilton House, Damien. Here everyone goes to school. Theresa will go with you and get you registered. Then she will see you to your first class. After that, it's up to you."

"I am *not* going to school," he stated adamantly. "People laugh at me and stare at me funny."

"They wouldn't laugh or stare if you'd do your exercises so you can get out of your wheelchair, Damien."

"If you try to make me go, I'll break this," he threatened as he picked up a small pottery vase containing a silk arrangement of flowers. Inwardly Jennifer cringed. The vase was a present from Tom, and even though its monetary value was minimal, its emotional value was irreplaceable. She took a chance and called his bluff. "Go ahead and break it, Damien. Break everything you can in this room. When you're done, you'll still go to school."

"You hate me!" he screamed.

"When you behave like this I do," she agreed.

He stared at her as if she'd just grown an extra eye. "You really hate me?" he asked in disbelief. "Why?"

"How would you feel if I went into your room at home and started breaking everything in sight? Would you like that?"

"No," he answered, and even though he was glowering at her, he replaced the vase. "But I'm still not going to school, and you can't make me. My dad won't let you make me.''

Jennifer tapped her foot impatiently on the throw rug spread across the gleaming hardwood floor. She was used to handling rebellious teenagers and had a hundred finely honed methods of dealing with them. But Damien was no more than a child, and she reluctantly admitted she wasn't certain what stance to take with him. A show of authority rarely worked with a runaway, but part of Damien's problem was a decided lack of authority. He had his father wrapped around his finger, and Trevor, as any parent in his position would respond, was more eager to pacify his son than to confront him.

"Fine, Damien. If you want to stay here and not go to school, then I expect you to remain in this room until bedtime. You will not be allowed to go outside with the other kids when they come home, nor will you be allowed to play any games. Roll your chair over into that corner, and I don't expect to see you move one inch the entire day, except to use the bathroom, of course. You may do that.''

His eyes were wide with confusion as he asked, "What about lunch?''

"Children who do not go to school don't need lunch. Now get into the corner, Damien.''

His eyes filled with tears, and he shook his head. "I'm not going to sit in the corner.''

"Are you going to school?''

"No.''

"Then you're going to sit in the corner until bedtime.''

"I'm going to call my dad and tell him you're being mean to me.''

"No, Damien," Jennifer stated firmly. "You are not going to call your father. He'll be here this evening, and you have my permission to tell him everything when he comes home. Until that time, you will not be allowed to disturb him. He is doing his job, and he doesn't need a spoiled brat calling and upsetting him."

"I'm not a spoiled brat!" he exclaimed as tears began to spill down his cheeks.

Jennifer closed her eyes and counted to twenty-five to gain control over her emotions. She wanted to grab him and hug him to her chest, but that action would not achieve the desired result. He had to realize from day one that she was the one in control. If she showed any leniency at all, she'd lose that battle.

She opened her eyes, now steeled against his tears, and ordered, "Get into the corner, Damien."

"I won't!"

"You will," Jennifer answered.

"No, I won't, and you can't make me!"

Jennifer clenched her fists at her sides and counted another twenty-five, but it did little to soothe her flaring temper. She walked over to the chair and bodily lifted him out of it. He started screaming and pounding at her with his fists. One punch landed firmly and split her lip, but Jennifer didn't even flinch. She carried him to the corner, settled him on the floor and turned away from him.

"I want my chair!" he screamed.

"Fine," she answered without glancing over her shoulder. She knew he had the strength to crawl to his chair if he wanted to. Whatever she did, she couldn't let him see the tears that had filled her eyes and were threatening to spill. "If you want it, go get it, Damien. Then, once you have it, get back into the corner.'' With those words, she walked out of the room.

"Jenny, are you all right?" Theresa questioned in concern as soon as Jennifer walked out into the hallway.

Jennifer swiped impatiently at the tears rolling down her cheeks and nodded. When she knew she had control of her voice again, she said, "Is steak good for a split lip?"

"You use steak for a black eye, Jenny."

"The little brat aimed too low."

Theresa tried to muffle her giggle, but it came out anyway, and Jennifer smiled through her tears. "I think I may have taken on more than I can handle, Theresa. I hate being a bad guy."

"You never did look good in a black hat," Theresa agreed. "Come on into the kitchen and put some ice on your lip. If we ever get him back on his feet, we'll enroll him in boxing lessons and prepare him for the Olympics."

"Little brat," Jennifer muttered as she obediently followed Theresa into the kitchen.

At lunchtime, Theresa once again stuck her head through the door. "Damien says he's hungry, Jenny. Should I feed him?"

"Has he made any move toward his wheelchair?"

"No. He hasn't moved an inch, and his bladder must be killing him."

"Tell him he can only have lunch if he can get to the kitchen."

"You're pushing him awfully hard, Jenny."

"Tell that to my lip," she grumbled, and raised her head.

"Oh, Jenny," Theresa commiserated. "Do you want me to bring you some more ice?"

"My lip is already frozen solid. I don't think any more ice will help."

"Maybe you need stitches."

"It's not *that* bad."

"Maybe not," Theresa said doubtfully. "I'll tell him he has to get to the kitchen on his own power."

"Thank you, Theresa."

It was only an hour or two later when a small voice spoke hesitantly from the doorway.

"Jenny, can I talk to you?"

Jennifer immediately spun her chair around to face her desk. She hadn't been able to concentrate on anything but the tug of will taking place between her and Damien, and she'd spent the time since lunch staring out the window.

"Of course, Angel, what is it?"

The girl gasped. "What happened to your lip?"

"Damien happened to it. What was it you wanted to talk about?"

"Damien," she whispered, and began to wring her hands. "He's crying, Jenny and . . . oh, after what he did to your lip, you won't care."

"I care, Angel," Jennifer assured the girl. She herself had had a difficult time resisting the boy's tears, and she had the distinct feeling that she'd just lost the war. "What's wrong with Damien?"

"He's hungry, and he has to go to the bathroom. He can't get to his chair, Jenny. Can I give it to him?"

"Yes," Jennifer sighed in defeat. Damien knew he was strong enough to crawl the six feet to the chair, but she'd never convince Angel of that. Angel would only believe that Jennifer was being unjustly cruel.

"Thank you, Jenny."

"You're welcome, Angel. Would you mind closing the door when you leave?"

"No. I'll close it."

"Thank you," Jennifer said, and spun back around to face the window.

So he'd won after all. She sighed wearily, popped two more aspirin into her mouth and leaned her head back against the chair. Tears welled into her eyes, and no matter how she tried to blink them back, she couldn't stop them from escaping. Finally she just gave in and allowed herself a good cathartic cry. For the first time in her life, she realized what her own mother had suffered before she'd run away from home. Monica had a lot of faults, but no one deserved this kind of torture.

Jennifer refused dinner when Theresa again stuck her head through the door, and Theresa closed it quietly behind her. The sun had set and the room was cloaked in darkness when the knock she'd been nervously anticipating finally came. It was strong and impatient, and Jennifer knew who it was before she called out an okay for entrance.

"Just what in hell were you trying to prove today?" Trevor roared as he threw open the door and stepped into the room. Then he stopped abruptly and frowned. "Jenny, why are you sitting in the dark?"

"I like the dark. What was it you wanted, Trevor?"

His anger was immediately renewed, overshadowing the strange, muffled quality of her voice. "I just talked to Damien, and he told me what you did to him today. Don't you ever do anything like that again, Jennifer."

"Fine, Trevor."

"I mean it, Jenny. He doesn't go to school because people make fun of him. I'll arrange for his tutor to start coming over here tomorrow."

"Fine, Trevor."

"And if Damien wants to call me, don't you ever deny him that right! I'm his father, Jennifer, and I'll talk to him whenever he wants to talk to me. Do you understand that?"

"Fine, Trevor."

"Just what in hell does 'Fine, Trevor' mean?" he exclaimed impatiently.

"Exactly that. Fine. In fact, since you seem to be such an expert on how he should be treated, why don't you just pack him up, stick him into your car and take him home? It will save us all a lot of trouble."

Trevor rocked back on his heels, stuffed his hands into the pockets of his suit pants and frowned at the back of the chair that faced him. If she'd delivered the words angrily, they probably never would have registered, but she'd delivered them in a low, dull voice that made them very succinct.

"Jenny, is something wrong?"

"What could possibly be wrong? You heard Damien's side of the story, came storming in here and gave me a piece of your mind. I've listened to what you have to say, and I've accepted it. Now do us all a favor and leave."

"You're going to give up on him just like that?"

"Just like that."

"Jenny, are you crying?"

"No."

"Are you sure? You sound funny."

"You would, too, if you had a split lip."

"A split lip?" Trevor echoed in concern. He closed the door behind him, flipped on the overhead light and moved toward her desk. "Jenny, turn around and look at me."

"No."

"Jenny, turn around," he repeated.

"Just get out of here, Trevor. And take that kid of yours with you."

"Jenny, please turn around and look at me."

"No. I want you to leave. Please turn out the light and close the door behind you."

"The hell I will," he swore angrily. He rounded the desk, grabbed the back of her chair and spun it toward him. He gasped in horror when he saw her lip. "Dear God, Jenny, what happened? Did you get mugged?"

"You could say that," she answered stiffly, and tried to spin the chair away from him.

He held on to the chair and knelt on the floor. "Let me look at it, Jenny. It looks as if you might need stitches."

"It's too late for stitches, Trevor. It happened hours ago. Now please leave my office."

"No." He raised gentle fingers to her lip. "Let me look at it, Jenny."

"Then look and get out of here," she responded in resignation and once again began to blink back tears.

"You *have* been crying," he stated quietly, brushing his fingers over a tear-stained cheek. "How did it happen, Jenny?"

"Why don't you ask Damien?"

"Damien did this to you?" he exclaimed in disbelief. "You're kidding me!"

"I don't kid, Trevor."

"Oh, Jenny." He sat back on his heels. "I am so sorry. He's never done anything like this before."

"Sure he has. Waterford crystal and fine china. This time it was just something a little more bruisable than breakable. But I'm as much to blame as he is. I lost my temper. I never should have lost my temper," she mumbled as she gazed blankly over his shoulder. "I never should have lost it," she repeated.

"It's very easy to lose your temper with him, Jenny. I know. I've been there," Trevor consoled her as he caught her cold hands between his warm ones and began to chafe them.

"But you're his father. I'm a psychologist. I shouldn't have lost my temper."

"Oh, baby," he sighed, leaning forward to pull her into his arms. "It's all right. It really is."

She would have sworn she'd cried all her tears, but still more surfaced, and she wrapped her arms around his neck, buried her face against his shoulder and began to sob anew. Trevor rocked her and pressed comforting kisses against her hair until the sobs began to subside.

"Let me look at your lip, Jenny," he once again requested.

She raised her head, and her hazel eyes were filled with despair. He brushed his fingers over her cheeks to wipe away her tears and smiled in understanding.

"You've never lost before, have you, Jenny?"

"No," she sniffed, "and I don't like it very much."

"We never do," he responded. "We're geared to succeed. I remember when I had my first professional failure, I swore I'd quit medicine. But after a good night's sleep, things looked better. Do you think you'd be willing to sleep on Damien and me for a night and see how you feel in the morning?''

"I doubt it would do any good. For the first time in my career, I feel inadequate. I don't think I'm capable of treating him, and we're probably all wasting our time."

"You're capable of treating him, Jenny. I'm afraid he has the Hawke stubbornness and explosive temper. He won the first battle today, but it was hardly Custer's Last Stand. You aren't going to let an eight-year-old kid ruin your perfect record, are you?"

"I thought you wanted to look at my lip," she complained, not quite willing to admit that he'd known exactly what words to use. There was no way she was going to let an eight-year-old boy get the best of her, and they both knew it.

"I do want to look at it."

He rose back up on his knees, tilted her head toward the light and examined her lip. "I think it's all right, Jenny. The tissue is bruised pretty badly, but the cut is fairly small. In a few days you're going to be good as new."

"Is that the doctor or the father talking?"

"A little of both." He leaned forward to press a butterfly kiss against her bruised lip. "There. Did that make it feel better?"

"That only works with mothers, Trevor."

"So think of me as a mother."

"Anatomically you'll never make it."

"Don't you have any imagination?"

"Not in this case."

He chuckled and tucked an errant curl behind her ear. "I'm sorry I came in here roaring at you, Jenny.

I promise that from now on I'll hear both sides before I let my temper get the best of me. Is it a deal?''

"Are you going to make Damien go to school?''

"Jenny, he can't handle ridicule. Wouldn't it be easier just to have the tutor come over?''

"Easier?'' she repeated. "Yes, Trevor, it would be easier, but it's not the best for Damien. If he's ridiculed enough, maybe he'll become angry, and if he becomes angry enough, maybe he'll walk. Protecting him isn't helping him—it's harming him. Giving in to his whims isn't going to make him walk. It's only going to encourage him to stay in that chair.''

Trevor released a long breath and rested his forehead against hers. "You're really pushing hard, lady.''

"We've both seen his legs, Trevor. I have to push hard. I don't want to see Damien confined to a wheelchair for the rest of his life any more than you do, but if we don't push hard, that's what's going to happen.''

"You're right, and I know you're right, Jenny, but it's very difficult. I don't like to see him traumatized, and when he looks up at me with tears in his eyes, I can't help but give in to him.''

"Now that's the father talking instead of the doctor. If he were a patient, would you be so lenient?''

He gave her a reluctant grin and shook his head. "No. I'd be riding his...tail so hard he wouldn't know what hit him.''

"You don't have to clean up your language for me, Trevor.''

"Sure I do. And I also have to clean up my son. By morning he's going to be convinced that Jennifer Hamilton is much more desirable to face than dear old Dad.''

"Don't be too hard on him, Trevor."

"I promise that his lip won't be any fatter than yours. Besides, he spoiled my fun!" he said with a wry smile. "I was looking forward to finishing what we started this morning, and now I'm going to have to take a rain check."

"I think it would be more appropriate to call it a lip check," she answered with a watery giggle.

"I don't care what it's called—it's still a check," he responded as he pulled her back into his arms and hugged her close. "We're a rowdy lot, but once you get to know us, we're pretty great guys, Jenny."

"Theresa's ready to enter Damien into the Olympic boxing championships."

"I'm ready to enter him into the sore bottom championships. How do you feel about corporal punishment?"

"With some kids it works, and with others it doesn't. I have a feeling Damien is a doesn't."

"I have a feeling you're right." He rested his cheek against her breast and listened to the steady beating of her heart. "I really did want to kiss you into oblivion tonight, Jenny."

"I really wanted you to, Trevor," she told him, and gently touched his hair. It felt so good to have a man holding her, comforting her, she admitted silently. She was strong, but she was human and needed the warmth of a human touch to make her complete.

Trevor ran his hands up her sides and turned his head to kiss the upper curve of her breast through the light blue cotton of her blouse. "Even the beating of your heart turns me on."

She smiled indulgently at his bent head and whimsically said, "It's beating just for you."

"That sounds almost Shakespearean."

"We could read *Romeo and Juliet* to each other some night."

"Forget the reading. Let's just act it out."

"Heathen!" She laughed.

"*Lecherous* would be a better description." He raised his hand and once again gently touched her lip. "I really am sorry about this, Jennifer."

"It's all right. I'll live."

"Do you still want us to leave?"

"No."

"You're sure?"

"Positive."

"I can promise you two things. In the morning Damien will be enrolled in school, and he'll never do something like this again. Okay?"

"Okay."

He raised his hand to his lips, pressed a kiss against his fingers and then touched them to her lips. "Good night, Jenny. Have sweet dreams."

"With a kiss like that, I couldn't have anything but sweet dreams."

"You're a marvel," he whispered. He kissed her forehead and left the office.

"I'm also in very great danger of falling in love," she admitted ruefully to the window after he'd gone.

A short time later, Trevor and Damien showed up at the office door.

"It's time for Damien to go to bed, Jennifer. If you're through for the night, of course."

"Of course," Jennifer said, raising her head.

Damien let out a cry of horror and brought his hands to his mouth as he looked at her face and the damage he'd done.

"Good night, Damien," Jennifer murmured as she walked out of the room.

She headed for the kitchen, which soon began to fill with kids as Trevor's and Damien's voices became louder and louder.

"That sounds like my dad," one of the kids muttered, then shot Jennifer a solicitous look. "But if I'd done that, Jenny, yelling at me isn't all he'd be doing."

"Damien didn't mean to hurt me," Jennifer explained. "He was angry, and it just happened."

"I've heard that story after a few black eyes," another kid commented dryly.

Theresa suddenly rose from her bent position in front of the stove, pulled out a new batch of cookies and ordered, "Everybody sit!"

Since Theresa's voice rarely held a note of authority, they all sat in surprise. She plopped the cookie sheet down on the cooling rack and shook her finger at the entire group.

"I don't want to hear anything more about Damien and what he's done. All of you have come into Hamilton House and given Jenny a bad time, even if you didn't hit her in the mouth. All of you are older than he, and none of you is in a wheelchair. The boy deserves a lecture from his father, and he's getting it. Jenny had to put up with all of you without any help from a father or a mother. Before you start throwing stones at that boy, you'd better be taking a good look at yourselves. Does anyone want a fresh cookie?" she finished.

Twenty guilty-looking faces nodded, and Jennifer almost laughed out loud. It was as if they were afraid to refuse Theresa's offer of a cookie.

When Trevor slammed out of Jennifer's office nearly an hour later, she was standing in the kitchen doorway. He looked grim, and she wanted to reach out and soothe the frown from his brow.

"We had a...talk," he told her.

"I heard. You're very...vocal."

"Sorry."

"Are you all right, Trevor?"

"Yes," he sighed.

"You're sure?"

He gave a weary nod. "Why does he always say he hates me?"

"Because he knows it will hurt."

"He's right. It does."

She wanted to pull him into her arms and hug him. Instead she said, "I think it's time you get some rest, Trevor. You've had an awfully long day."

"Are you sending me to my room?" he questioned with a grin.

"Do you need to be sent to your room?"

"Yes, and so do you, Jennifer. You've been up as long as I have, and you have a few more battle scars to prove it."

"He really didn't mean to hurt me, Trevor. He'd never purposely hurt me."

"Purposely or not, he did it, Jenny. I will tolerate many things from my son, but that is not one of them. I think he understands that."

"Trevor?"

"Yes."

"Could I have a hug?"

"Oh, Jenny," he said, and swept her up into his arms.

* * *

There were two things in the world Jennifer loved and could never get enough of. One was peaches and the other was sleep. The emotionally trying day had exhausted her, and she crawled into bed with a weary sigh, but it seemed as if her head had barely touched the pillow before there was a knock on the door. She wanted to pull the pillow over her head and tell whoever it was to go away. Instead she yawned, sat up and called for entrance.

The door opened, and Angel stood silhouetted in the hall light, looking forlorn and very young and vulnerable in her long cotton nightgown.

"Jenny, Damien had a nightmare, and I can't make him stop crying."

"I'm coming," Jennifer said, and climbed out of bed.

"I tried, Jenny," Angel sighed as they walked together toward the stairs.

"I know you did," Jennifer assured her, wrapping an arm around the girl's shoulders. She gave her a comforting hug. "It's not your job to make him stop crying, honey. It's mine. The reason you're downstairs with him is that you can come get me if he needs me. You did the right thing."

"I feel so sorry for him," Angel responded, leaning her head against Jennifer's shoulder. "I wish he could walk."

"Well, that's exactly what we're going to try to make him do. In fact, tomorrow evening his physical therapist is going to come over and show me the exercises Damien needs to do every day. How would you like to watch and then help me make sure he does them?"

"Will they help make him walk?"

"They'll strengthen his legs so that he has a better chance, but I'm afraid Damien doesn't like to do them."

"Do they hurt him?"

"Some of the exercises are probably a little uncomfortable, but it would be worth a little pain if you knew you'd be able to walk in the end, don't you think?"

"Yes, and I'll make sure he does them every day, Jenny. I promise," Angel vowed fervently.

"We'll work together to make sure he does."

"I love you, Jenny," Angel told her.

"I love you, too, sweetheart."

Damien's cot was in a corner of Jennifer's office, and she entered the room and sat down on its edge, gently touching the sobbing boy's hair.

"It was just a dream, Damien. You're all right."

He sat up abruptly and threw himself into her arms, showing a mobility of limbs that Jennifer knew he'd never display if he weren't so upset. He was even stronger than she'd imagined, and she felt her heart soar. If they could get him to exercise, he'd recover very fast. She just knew it.

"Don't hate me, Jenny," he cried piteously.

"I don't hate you, Damien."

"You said you did."

"I guess I did, but I don't hate *you*. I hate the way you sometimes behave. There's a big difference. Do you want to tell me about your dream?"

"No."

"It might make you feel better if you did."

"I can't," he whispered, and he buried his head between her breasts.

"Was the dream about your mother?"

He nodded and clung to her more desperately. "I miss her, Jenny. I want her to come home."

"I know," she said, rocking him.

"She just sat in the car and kept staring straight ahead. I yelled and yelled and yelled, but she wouldn't talk to me."

Tears welled in Jennifer's eyes, and she ran a hand soothingly up and down his back, making a mental note to ask Trevor how long Damien had been trapped in the car before help had arrived. Every minute would have seemed like hours, and since he had suffered a spinal injury, he probably hadn't been able to move. His natural response would have been to call to his mother for help, but she had died instantly.

The memory of her own father's death hit her with such force that bile rose to her throat and she had to swallow hard to keep it back. The nightmares never completely went away. You simply learned to live with them.

"We're going to do something very special now, okay, Damien?"

"What are we going to do?"

"We're going to go to a magic place. I want you to close your eyes and listen very hard to what I say. Do you think you can do that?"

"I don't know." He sniffed.

"I bet you can. Will you try?"

He nodded.

"Good. Now close your eyes and imagine that we're walking up a little path and we see a whole bunch of big trees ahead of us. They're so tall that it looks as if they touch the sky. Can you see them?" She smiled when he nodded, his eyes so tightly closed that his brow was furrowed. "I knew you could. We're getting closer to them, and a great big robin with the reddest breast you ever saw just flew out of that corner tree. I can't believe he's so big, can you?''

Damien shook his head and then buried it back against her breast. She tenderly stroked his hair. "He's flying all over the sky, and now he's going behind the trees. Let's go see what he's doing."

"Yeah," Damien whispered. "I want to see what he's doing."

"Okay, but we have to hurry or he might fly off!"

"Let's run."

"Okay. We're running, and now we're almost there. We just passed the first tree and the second and...oh, my. Look at that, Damien! He's sitting in the middle of a beautiful meadow, and he's catching a worm. I bet he has babies to feed."

"I bet he does, too! Can we see his nest?"

"I bet we can. Oh, sure enough, there it is. It's up in the tallest tree. Almost at the top! Boy, he wanted to make sure nothing could climb up and get his babies, didn't he?"

"Yeah," Damien whispered in awe. "Not even a cat could climb that high!"

"You're right. Not even a cat could climb that high. He's a real smart daddy, isn't he?"

"Just like my daddy. If we had to live in a nest, he'd make sure no cat could get me."

"You're darn right he'd make sure no cat could get you. That's why it's always very important to do exactly what your daddy tells you to do. It's a daddy's job to make sure his babies are safe, and you never want to make his job hard, right?"

"Right," Damien agreed. "My dad loves me."

"He loves you so much, Damien, that sometimes it makes his heart hurt."

"Especially when I'm bad, huh?" he questioned with astounding insight.

"Yes, Damien, especially when you're bad."

"He yelled at me tonight."

She sighed and rested her cheek against the top of his head. "He yelled at you because he loves you, Damien, and he wants to see you be the best that you can be."

"I told him I hate him, but I don't really hate him," he confessed, a single tear rolling down his cheek. "I love him, Jenny."

"I know you do, and he knows it, too, but just for good measure, why don't you give him a big kiss and a big hug in the morning and tell him you love him? Sometimes daddies need to be reassured. They have an awfully hard job."

"Okay."

"Do you think you can go back to sleep now?"

"Uh-huh, but will you stay here for a while?"

"Yes, Damien, I'll stay here for a while."

"Thank you, Jenny. I'm sorry I hit you today. I didn't mean to hurt you."

"I know you didn't Damien, and I accept your apology. Now go back to sleep."

He curled into a ball and clung to her hand. Jennifer smiled down at him and brushed his hair back from his forehead.

She didn't see the large shadow that loomed in the doorway, and Trevor turned away as he swallowed the lump in his throat and brushed the tears from his cheeks. He'd awakened suddenly, sensing that something was wrong with Damien, but Jenny had already been with him. He'd quietly stood there listening as she comforted his son, and he knew that he had never been so deeply touched in his life.

Chapter Five

The next morning, Damien was true to his word. He hugged his father, gave him a big kiss and told him he loved him. Trevor hugged him back so hard that Damien began to protest that he couldn't breathe. Trevor glanced up at Jennifer and gave her a smile so brilliant that her heart expanded until it pressed against her ribs.

Trevor insisted on taking Damien to school and registering him himself, and Jennifer reluctantly agreed. The public school system that served Hamilton House was a far cry from Beverly Hills, but it did provide a good education. Most of the morning she eyed the telephone warily, expecting Trevor to call and inform her that his son would not be attending *that* school. But the call never came.

The remainder of the week continued at a hectic pace, and much to Jennifer's chagrin, there were no more passionate interludes between her and Trevor. Every time she saw him, the longing to be in his arms became more insistent, but he was on call and seemed to live at the hospital. Her own demanding duties kept her going from dawn until nearly midnight, when she'd finally collapse into bed and try to get some sleep.

Damien began to fall into Hamilton House's schedule, and he and Angel were becoming inseparable. When he'd refused to do his exercises, Angel had scolded him until tears ran down his cheeks. Now they were working together, and he was doing his exercises two and sometimes three times a day. His physical therapist was ecstatic, but Damien still refused to try to stand, and not even Angel could convince him to attempt it.

Jennifer had also begun to pick up on a subtle nuance in his speech pattern as she counseled him. On the rare occasions she could get him to discuss his mother, he always spoke of her in the present tense. It hadn't taken her long to realize that Damien had not really accepted his mother's death.

Consultations with his former counselor and conversations with Trevor convinced her that Damien somehow felt his mother would return someday if he remained in his wheelchair. She knew that that conviction was going to be difficult to challenge, especially since Damien had been too ill to attend his mother's funeral, which might have helped him conceptualize death.

When Saturday came, Jennifer closed the door on her office, determined to ignore the stack of papers and charts on her desk, and joined the kids in a rip-roaring basketball game on the cracked pavement in front of Hamilton House. It had rained earlier, and the sun came out with a ferociousness that only Los Angeles could experience in February. The resultant humidity soon had perspiration dewing her face and her sleeveless T-shirt clinging to her damply.

She and Racer faced each other as he dribbled the ball, trying to decide how to maneuver around her. She waited patiently until he glanced away. Then she raced in, stole the ball, dribbled it the length of the small court and slam-dunked it. She let out a startled gasp of surprise when she came down on her feet and her back came into firm contact with what felt suspiciously like a very wide, very bare chest.

"Hi," Trevor murmured when she turned around.

She gulped at the sight of him standing there with no shirt and a pair of worn jeans that hung so low on his hips that she wondered why they didn't fall off. He wrapped an arm around her waist and pulled her off the concrete.

"Hi, yourself," she answered as she self-consciously brushed back the damp hair that clung to her face. "What are you doing here? I thought you were on call."

"I was, but my partner has a critically ill patient and wanted to hang around the hospital. He agreed to take my call for the weekend."

"Oh."

"You're pretty good."

"What?"

"Good, Jennifer. At basketball," he qualified with a chuckle.

"Oh. Yeah, I guess I am. It's good exercise."

"So that's your secret," he said, and she shivered as his gaze moved down her in a lazy appraisal that set her senses spinning. "Something really strange happened to me on the drive home."

"It did?"

"Uh-huh. I was driving past this parking lot, and I heard this little voice say, 'I want to go to the beach.'"

"Do you hear these voices often, Trevor?" she questioned with a teasing grin.

"I've never heard one before. I guess that's why I was so surprised. I pulled over to the curb and looked up, and guess what I saw."

"A giant bumblebee with a wingspan as wide as the Golden Gate Bridge."

He laughed in delight. "No, but you're close. It is yellow and has a few black stripes on it."

"It does?"

"Yep."

"What was it?"

"A bus."

"A bus?" she echoed.

"A bus big enough to haul the entire population of Hamilton House to the beach."

"Really?"

"Yep. I rented it and a driver and brought it home."

"You rented a bus and a driver, Trevor?"

"Yes. I thought we'd take it to the beach and try it out. If you really like it, I'll buy it for you."

"Buy it for me? You can't buy me a bus, Trevor."

"Couldn't you use a bus?"

"I suppose, but I can't let you buy us a bus."

"Why not?"

"Well, because...I can't. Buses are too expensive."

"What are you charging me for Damien's care?"

"Nothing."

"And for our room and board?"

"Nothing."

"Well, in that case, I can buy you a bus. Want to go to the beach so we can try it out?"

"It's pretty late, Trevor. By the time we got the kids ready and some food packed . . ."

"The food's already on board. When the bus was rolling down the street, I heard this other little voice cry, 'You have to buy me or I'll be thrown out at the end of the day.' Lo and behold, that little voice came from a deli."

"It seems to be your day for voices," she said with another grin.

"What can I say?" he asked, and threw his arms up in the air in a helpless gesture. "Are we going to the beach or not?"

"You'll have to ask the president and vice president. They approve or disapprove of all outings."

He stuck two fingers into his mouth and let out a whistle so shrill that Jennifer clapped her hands over her ears. He immediately got results, however, and Jennifer decided she'd have him teach her the trick. She'd never heard the group become silent so quickly.

"I have rented a bus for the day," Trevor announced. "What would all of you think about going to the beach?"

The resultant roar left little doubt that in a democratic society—which, of course, Hamilton House was—the vote was unanimous.

Trevor gave a pleased nod and said, "You have ten minutes to get into your swimsuits and onto the bus. Anyone not present will be left behind."

Jennifer had also never seen the group move so swiftly. "You have quite a technique, Trevor."

"Jennifer, I wouldn't touch that line with a ten-foot pole," he said with a chuckle. He wrapped an arm around her waist and began leading her toward the house. "You do have a bathing suit, don't you?"

"Sure."

"I certainly hope it's a bikini."

"Why?"

"The more I can ogle, the more I like."

"That's what I love about the filthy rich. They're always so eager to indulge themselves in decadence."

He stopped abruptly, caught her chin in his hand and tilted her head upward. "Jennifer, that sounded suspiciously like an insult."

Guilty, she tried to duck her head, but he held it in place. "I'm sorry, Trevor."

"I can't help my financial status. I was born rich—I don't deny that—but that doesn't mean there's something wrong with me."

"Of course it doesn't," she mumbled, once again trying to duck her head. He didn't release her.

"Do you know what I think?" he asked.

"No," she answered.

"I think we need to have some time alone so we can talk. How about a long walk along the beach?"

"It depends."

"On what?"

"On whether or not Theresa wants to come. I can't leave the kids alone."

"That's reasonable," he replied agreeably. "But if Theresa comes, you owe me a walk."

"If she comes, you have one."

Theresa chose that moment to race out the door, clearly determined to be the first one on the bus. She wore a gigantic straw hat and carried three bottles of sunscreen.

"Last one in is a rotten egg!" she called out gaily as she ran for the bus.

"You heard the woman," Trevor said, and gave a fond pat to Jennifer's posterior. "Get your suit, Jenny, and get on that bus!"

"I think you were a drill sergeant in an earlier life, Trevor." Then she asked, "What about Damien? Does he have a suit?"

"I stopped by the house and picked it up. I'll get him changed and onto the bus. All you have to worry about is you."

"Boy, that's a change," she said with a sigh.

"I know." He tweaked the end of her nose. "Today is going to be 'give Jenny a rest day.' You've definitely earned it."

"You're an awfully nice man, Trevor Hawke."

"I know," he repeated ingenuously, "but I think you bring out the best in me." He glanced down at the slim gold watch on his wrist and shook his head. "You only have six minutes, Jenny. If you aren't on that bus, we're leaving without you."

"That's what you think!" she exclaimed, and she ran into the house.

Jennifer was the last person on the bus, and Trevor had extended her six minutes to twelve and a half. She would have been on time, but she'd forgotten where she'd stashed her swimsuit—a bikini more than a decade old. She'd pulled on clean shorts and a top to cover the revealing garments, but she still flushed, feeling as if Trevor had X-ray vision when he winked at her suggestively as she dropped into the front seat beside Damien.

Damien smiled at her and asked, "Do you like seashells, Jenny?"

"I love seashells," she answered. "In fact, I have a big collection of them. Remind me when we get back, and I'll show it to you."

"Oh," he said, sounding disappointed. "I was going to collect some for you."

"I always need more," she assured him, lacing her fingers with his.

She turned toward the group and soon had a singing marathon started. They sang every camp song that anyone could remember until they arrived at the beach. The driver parked the bus, and Trevor began giving orders for the unloading. He'd thought of everything. There was a large supply of blankets, enough food to feed the entire group three times over and skewers for roasting hot dogs and marshmallows.

A good twenty minutes had passed before the bus had been unloaded and the goods settled into a convenient spot. Theresa and Angel took Damien in tow and pushed him down to the ocean, helping him out of his wheelchair and into the water so he could float under their careful supervision.

"It's our turn now," Trevor suddenly said in a husky voice behind her. "Turn around, Jenny."

Slowly she obeyed, her eyes wide and expectant. He grinned and began to unbutton the shirt he'd pulled on before they'd left. She gulped as she watched him reveal his wide, tantalizingly smooth chest. He slipped the shirt off his shoulders and dropped it to the ground carelessly. Her eyes fastened themselves on his fingers as he undid the snap on his jeans and then lowered the zipper.

"Have you ever thought of doing this as a sideline?" she questioned hoarsely as he began to ease his jeans down over his hips. "I understand there are some good male strip clubs around here and that the career can be very lucrative."

He chuckled, dropped his pants, and Jennifer clasped her hands together, praying that her knees wouldn't give way. He had on the briefest pair of swimming trunks she'd ever seen, and they very clearly displayed his every masculine attribute.

"Your turn, Jenny," he said in a throaty whisper.

She nodded and raised trembling hands to her blouse. It seemed to take forever to get those disobedient buttons out of their holes, but she finally managed to release them and mimicked Trevor's action by dropping her shirt to the ground.

"Oh, boy." His eyes glued themselves to her ample breasts, which strained against the almost non-existent orange top confining them.

Then his gaze dropped to watch her unzip her jeans, and he released a gust of air as she slid them down over her hips, revealing every lush, feminine curve that until now he'd only been able to imagine.

"Well, what do you think?" she asked hesitantly.

"That if you lower your eyes while looking at me, you're in for the shock of your life." He grabbed her hand and began dragging her after him. "I think it's time for our walk."

"We should tell someone where we're going, Trevor."

"We will when we know ourselves," he answered tightly, picking up his pace.

"Just what does that mean, Trevor?"

"That if you don't keep your mouth shut, I'm going to kiss it shut and then do some very ungentlemanly things to you. Just be quiet for a while and walk, okay?"

"Okay," she agreed, and fell into step beside him. It had to be sinful to feel so pleased that she could affect him in this manner, but the feminine side of her nature felt no remorse.

They continued to walk together silently until they'd rounded a far bend and entered a small deserted stretch of beach. Trevor's pace slackened, and they walked a little farther before he stopped, dropped her hand and picked up a small seashell, which he tossed toward the water.

"I am Reginald Hawke's son," he stated unnecessarily.

"I know that, Trevor."

"Do you also know how hard it was to grow up in his shadow?"

"I have an idea."

"Having an idea of how it was and knowing how it was are two different things, Jennifer. My father loved me—still does, for that matter—but he was a very busy, very hard and very demanding man. He worked like a demon for everything he has, and he expected that same kind of dedication from everyone around him. And I mean everyone, Jennifer. My mother and my two sisters suffered right along with me. But I will give him one thing. He didn't care if you won or lost, only that you gave it your best shot. It's a quality I had hoped to instill in my own son, although it appears I may have missed that mark."

"You haven't missed, Trevor. Right now you're dealing with a whole new set of rules."

He nodded and tossed another shell out into the water. "I went through a period of hating my father. I think most adolescents do, but it wasn't really him I hated. It was his money. Do you know how many people want to be your friend when they find out your father is *the* Reginald Hawke?"

"Yes," Jennifer answered, and tossed her own shell out into the ocean. "A few more than want to be your friend when they find out you're the only heir to Michael O'Brien's fortune."

"That's right." Trevor arched his brow slightly at the first reference she'd ever made to her wealthy past. "When I was a boy, I once heard my father call a man a human leech, but I never understood what he meant until I got older. One of the reasons my wife and I married was that we came from the same background. Neither of us was losing or gaining anything of monetary value by marrying. We were equals in that sense, and neither of us had to worry about being used for our money. We didn't have the ... best of marriages, but both of us could have had much worse."

He sighed and turned those expressive violet eyes on her. There was a hint of both anger and pain in them when he said, "I was blessed with the dubious honor of being born to wealth, Jennifer, and I resent it when someone casts a stone at me for it even in jest. I'm wealthy. I'll always be wealthy. But I try to think that the man inside is even wealthier."

"I sincerely apologize for offending you earlier," Jennifer responded. "I never thought about it until just now, but maybe I have a kind of prejudice against rich people. An odd prejudice, when you consider the fact that I'm very wealthy myself. I don't have full access to my money and never will. My father always feared that some unscrupulous man might come along and snap me up, so he put my money in trust so that unscrupulous man could never get his hands on it. I get a healthy check once a month, and every penny of that check is spent on Hamilton House."

"Every penny?" Trevor echoed incredulously. "Surely you've established yourself as a nonprofit organization and solicit donations."

"We're established as a nonprofit organization, but I don't solicit donations. We do get a few state checks every month for some of the kids who were state charges before they came to us, and I do accept a few checks from the well-to-do families whose children live with us."

"Well-to-do?" Trevor gasped, and glanced back the way they'd come, even though he knew he couldn't see the group. "Some of those kids are from wealthy families?"

"Economics has nothing to do with runaways, Trevor. Kids from all backgrounds run away. I'm very lucky at Hamilton House because I've been able to contact most of the kids' parents and assure them that they're all right. Some of my colleagues aren't that lucky. The kids refuse to tell them who they are because they fear they'll be sent home."

"But why don't you take donations?" Trevor asked in confusion.

"Because when people start to give you money," she explained, "they also start giving you help. Once they start helping, they always know a better way, and because they've given you money, they're offended if you don't do it *their* way. I have enough trouble keeping up with the kids. I don't need to play politics at the same time."

"It sounds to me as if you might be cutting off your nose to spite your face, Jennifer. You could always hire additional staff to help with the kids."

"Now you sound like my mother," she said, chuckling. "I guess it's true when they say great minds think alike. But right or wrong, I've got to do it my way."

He smiled and shook his head. "How could you walk away from affluence and take up your life at Hamilton House? Don't you ever miss the luxuries you had?"

"I miss a few of them," Jennifer admitted, "but I never really fit into that kind of life. My mother tried hard to make me fit into it, but it just didn't take. My dad always said I was a throwback to his rough-and-ready heritage, and it kind of looks like he was right."

"Well, personally, I kind of like the rough-and-ready lady," Trevor said as he caught her around the waist and swung her toward him. "How's your lip?"

"I don't know," she said breathlessly as she came into firm contact with his hard length. She slipped her tongue out and traced the contour of her lower lip. "It feels kind of...numb."

"Numb? Hmm, that sounds serious. I think I should check it out, don't you?"

"It does sound like a consultation is in order."

"My fee is high."

"It is? Do you take credit cards?"

"No, but for you, I'll take it out in trade."

"Trade? What kind of trade?"

"We'll talk payment after I've checked out the area in question."

"Can't I at least get an estimate?"

"Gladly," he growled, and pulled her hips against him.

"Trevor!" she gasped. "I think you need a cold shower!"

"I've been taking them all week, and it hasn't done me a bit of good," he confessed, and he caught her lips in a hungry kiss that made her feel as if she were being devoured.

His hand slid down to her breast, and he cupped it, stroking his thumb across its peak until she was straining urgently against him.

"Trevor, it's a public beach," she reminded him when he let her come up for a quick breath of air. "Someone might see us."

"That shark cruising around out there doesn't get much entertainment, and we have to keep him occupied so he doesn't eat the kids."

He was lowering her to the sand, and although she gave a negative shake of her head, she didn't make any other effort to stop him. "Trevor, one of the kids might come looking for us," she said tremulously when he lowered himself over her and rotated his hips against her, once again giving her ample proof of his aroused state.

"I'll tell them you fainted and that I'm giving you mouth-to-mouth resuscitation."

"After hearing my lectures on the chickens and frogs, they'll never believe that, Trevor."

"Sounds like a pretty graphic lecture to me. I'll have to sit in and listen the next time you give it. Lord, I want you, Jenny."

"That's pretty evident."

"You're always so quick with a comeback."

"Self-preservation. It's a must when you live with a houseful of teenagers. By the way, how was my lip?"

"Mmm. It needs a little therapy."

"It does?"

"Uh-huh." He lowered his head, capturing her bottom lip between his lips and sucking on it gently.

Her reaction was instantaneous. She groaned low in her throat and arched her hips urgently toward him, murmuring in protest when he teasingly pulled away from her.

With a contented sigh, he lifted his head and smiled down at her while his fingers traced the contour of her cheek.

"What are you thinking?" she asked, her lips curving up in a tender smile.

"I'm just daydreaming."

"About what?"

"I'm not so sure I should tell you."

"Why not?"

"Well, a man should have a few private fantasies, shouldn't he?"

"No, he should not," she answered, running a finger along his lower lip. "Tell me your fantasy."

He shook his head.

"Come on, tell me," she urged. "I'd like to share it. Besides, we have to do something to keep that shark out there occupied."

He chuckled, and she let out a sigh of bliss when he lowered his hips back to her. "I was imagining that it's night, Jenny."

"All right, it's night. What kind of night is it?"

"A hot night. Even the breeze blowing in off the ocean is hot. It's the kind of heat wave that makes you feel like you're burning up inside."

His description was delivered in a soft, mesmerizing whisper and seemed so real that Jennifer's tongue automatically flicked out to wet hot, parched lips. His eyes flared brightly as they followed the action.

There was a vibrant, husky tone to his voice when he resumed his fantasy. "We've come here to cool off, but even after a swim, the breeze has us hot again in just a few moments. We're alone, and the moon is shining down on us. You begin to pull at your bikini top. It feels sticky and clammy. You can hardly bear to have it touching you."

Jennifer began to shift uncomfortably beneath him and actually had the urge to tug at her top.

"I'm watching you, and tell you to take your suit off. After all, it's just us out here. But you're shy, and you tell me I have to take mine off, too. I agree, but we can't decide who's going to go first, so we stand up and face each other and slowly—so very slowly, Jenny—we peel those clammy garments away. You look like a goddess standing there in the moonlight, your copper hair slicked to your head and the copper curls at your thighs gleaming in the moonlight, beckoning to me, inviting me to discover their hidden treasure."

Jennifer's breasts began to heave in response to his erotic words.

"Then, like a maiden, you let your eyes drift over me, and you gasp when you see how ready I am for you. I'm burning for you with a fire that's ten times hotter than the heat wave we'd come here to escape. You stand poised, afraid to stay but not wanting to leave. I know that all I have to do is step forward and you'll be in my arms, but I want you to make that choice. I want you to come to me because you want to come. I just stand there, looking at you and begging you with my eyes. You turn and take several paces toward the water and then look back at me. I can see that you're still torn, but suddenly you call out my name and race toward me, flinging yourself into my arms with such force that we tumble to the sand."

Jennifer was now breathing shallowly, and her hips automatically rotated beneath him, causing him to emit a low, masculine growl of approval.

"You're so eager for me now, Jenny. You're lying on top of me, and I can barely contain myself as you brush your satin flesh against me. I want to bury myself in you and put out the fire, but you're like a rare fine wine. You need to be savored slowly to be truly enjoyed. I roll, pulling you beneath me. You protest, but I ignore you. I kiss you here," he whispered and pressed a light, feathery kiss at the top of her forehead, "and then I rain kisses over every inch of your face until I finally arrive here."

He fleetingly kissed the corner of her lips, and Jennifer shifted her head, trying to capture his mouth in a real kiss.

"Feel how eager you are for me, Jenny?"

"Kiss me, Trevor!" she demanded urgently.

"Oh, yes, love. I'm going to kiss you. I'm going to kiss you everywhere now. I avoid your lips, knowing that their honey will capture me and I'll lose my will. Instead I lower my head to here."

His hand once again cupped her breast, and Jennifer moaned and arched, pressing it firmly into his hand. His thumb began to stroke the peak as he now whispered, "I rain tiny kisses all around it, Jenny, and you catch your breath and hold it in anticipation." Jennifer did just that. "Finally, when you feel you can't stand it a moment longer, I settle my lips around your nipple and draw it gently into my mouth. You go wild beneath me, Jenny. I've never experienced such wildness in a woman.

"Again I almost lose control, and I draw away from your breast. I'm breathing raggedly. My heart is pounding, and I can feel the blood racing through my veins. I know I'm going to have to give up the game. I have to take you, but suddenly your other breast catches my eye, and I know that I have to have a taste of it first. The torture begins all over."

His hand shifted to her other breast, and Jennifer closed her eyes tightly and caught her bottom lip between her teeth.

"You are torturing me, Trevor," she whispered. "I can't stand this. We have to stop."

"We will, but we have to make love first, Jenny. Just listen to me. I've finally finished with your other breast, and I ease slightly away from you. It's time now. Your thighs have parted, inviting my entrance, but there's so much left of you that I haven't explored, and I have to explore you. I have to know every inch of the beautiful exterior before I can lose myself in the velvety inner heat of you. My lips begin to travel lower and lower, and I—"

"Trevor!" she gasped, clutching his upper arms. "Stop this—now! I can't stand any more!"

She gazed up at him with tear-filled eyes that reflected the desire that was eating her alive. He smiled down at her tenderly and brushed a tear from her lower lashes. "All right, love, we'll stop."

She groaned and nuzzled his chest. "I think I'm dying, Trevor."

"It's a curable malady, Jennifer," he told her as he stood and lifted her into his arms and began to stride toward the ocean.

"Trevor, you're going to have to let me go," she told him, needing to put some distance between them.

"Never." He lowered his head to capture her lips in a searing kiss.

He finally stopped when he'd waded out to where the water came halfway up his chest, and he let her slide down his length into the cold, refreshing water, keeping his arm firmly around her waist.

"Feeling better?" he asked solicitously.

Her eyes shot open when her body collided with his and she once again became aware of his passion.

"I'm certainly cooled off, but I'm not certain about you, Trevor."

"I'm fine, Jenny."

"Are you sure?" she asked doubtfully.

"I'm sure. Just holding you in my arms makes me feel wonderful. Thank you for letting me share my fantasy."

"Oh, Trevor," she sighed. "How did someone born so filthy rich turn out to be such a nice man?"

He chuckled and said tongue-in-cheek, "I guess I was just born with a heart of gold, Jenny."

"Oh, you!" She laughed and pushed herself away from him. "I'm going back to shore. You follow only when you're presentable."

"You're going to leave me alone out here with that shark?" he asked in mock alarm.

"Yes, and don't let him take a bite out of anything you can't spare."

"Oh, don't worry, Jenny. I'm not about to let anything happen to me until we live out our little fantasy."

Jennifer gulped as the flames of desire began to flare once again. She turned away from him without a word and made her way back to the beach, where she dropped down onto the sand and buried her face in her hands.

He'd delivered the words like a man making a vow, and suddenly she was frightened. She was frightened because she knew that if she ever let him make love to her, she'd be *in* love, and as she'd told him in the beginning, it was an impossible love. She'd never believed in the old saying that absence makes the heart grow fonder, and once Hamilton House moved to the country, she'd definitely be absent. They'd have to be satisfied with an affair that would eventually grow cold, because for love to survive, there had to be a commitment.

She raised her head and gazed longingly out over the water, watching Trevor swim back and forth in long, powerful strokes. Mentally she flipped a coin. Tails she'd have the affair. Heads she wouldn't. The coin was still in the air when he came striding out of the water, and she let it stay there.

Chapter Six

Trevor smiled when he reached Jennifer's side, and she returned his smile. He offered a hand, and she took it, letting him pull her to her feet. He wrapped an arm around her shoulders, tucking her close to his side, and they walked back along the beach in pensive silence.

Even though the day was warm, it was still February and the water was cold. The kids had stopped swimming. Some were playing Frisbee, and another group lounged on blankets in the sun. Theresa was leaning against a rock with her hat pulled down over her eyes as if she were sleeping, but Jennifer knew that the woman was wide-awake and aware of where each child was at every moment.

Her gaze shifted to the back of Damien's wheelchair, set next to Theresa. With the sun in her eyes,

Jennifer couldn't see the boy, but she assumed he was happily sunbathing slouched in the chair.

Then Trevor exclaimed, "Jennifer, Damien's sitting on the ground!"

"What?" She followed his pointing finger. "Well, I'll be," she said when she spotted the boy, sitting on the sand next to Angel and helping her build a sand castle. "I wonder how she got him to do that?"

"How does she get him to do anything?" Trevor questioned in wonder. "She seems to have a magic touch with him. I wish I could learn her secret."

"It's called love, Trevor."

"I love him, Jennifer."

"It's a different kind of love. Angel is fulfilling a dream through Damien, and she isn't about to let him take away that dream."

"What's her story?"

"She comes from a very large family. For years she was the only girl, and she wanted a baby sister. Finally she got her wish. Unfortunately her sister was born with a congenital spinal defect and has never been able to walk. Angel convinced herself that the reason her sister couldn't walk was that her family couldn't afford to get her proper medical care. There were just too many mouths to feed. So she decided that if they didn't have to feed *her*, they could use that money to help her sister. She ran away."

Jennifer smiled sadly before continuing. "But there's no help for the girl. I got a copy of the medical records and took Angel to three different surgeons, who all patiently explained to her that her sister would never walk. She's accepted it in her way, but she still wants to have hope. With Damien she has real hope, and I'm praying that once we get him onto his feet, she'll finally go home. Her family misses her very much."

Trevor shook his head. "You know, it just goes to show how wrong we can be about things. I've always thought runaways were kids who were abused or neglected, but that's not necessarily true, is it?"

"No," Jennifer answered. "Children run away for different reasons. Some of these kids do come from abusive families and were running away from very real problems. Others were running away from very real *imagined* problems. There are even a few out there who run away just as an act of defiance—I'm-grown-up-now-and-I-can-be-my-own-boss type of thing. Then they end up out there in a big scary world, and they don't know where to turn. That's where places like Hamilton House come in. The kids are granted sanctuary, and people like me work with them."

"If you find out who they are, don't you feel obligated to force them to go back to their families?" Trevor questioned. "If Damien ran away, I would insist that he come home. I couldn't stand by and let him become someone else's responsibility."

Jennifer's eyes flared with impatience. "And what happens if I force him to go home before he's ready, Trevor? Do you put a full-time guard on him to make sure he doesn't run away again? Because that's exactly what he'd do. I do process a lot of kids who stay with me a week or two, and then I return them to their families. They enter counseling together and work their problems out. Other kids I know won't stay if I send them back home, and the next time they run away, they won't be so quick to seek sanctuary. They were turned in once, and they're not going to let it happen again. We both know the dangers out there,

Trevor. I'd much rather have them with me and deal with unhappy parents than have them out on the streets without any protection."

"I love the fire in your eyes when you get on your soapbox," he told her with a grin, and ran his finger down the length of her nose.

She blushed, and ducked her head. He chucked her affectionately under the chin.

"For what it's worth, Jennifer, I understand what you're saying, and I have to agree with you. But how in the world did you get into this business in the first place?"

Jennifer frowned and curled her toes into the sand. "That's a very long story, Trevor, and I have neither the inclination nor the desire to discuss it right now."

"I see." He glanced away from her, but not before she'd seen the hurt in his eyes. "I thought we were getting close enough that you'd want to share a few personal things with me. I guess I was wrong."

"Trevor..." She gazed at him sadly when he shrugged away from the hand she laid on his arm.

"I think I'll play some Frisbee," he said, and he left her side.

"Oh, boy," she muttered, and she released a sigh.

She hadn't meant to hurt his feelings. He'd caught her off guard with the question, and she'd instinctively known he wouldn't be satisfied with her pat answer. He'd want the entire story. It was still very difficult for her to discuss that two-year period of her life following her father's death. As she'd told Edward, she'd buried her guilt, but she had never completely resolved it. The fire on the boat had been her fault. Since they had been several miles out at sea, her father had thrown her overboard but remained behind to send out a distress call. He hadn't had time to get off before the explosion.

It had taken the Coast Guard an hour to respond to his distress call, and she'd floated in the water with the thousands of shattered remnants, grieving for her father and knowing she'd never see him again.

Tears filled her eyes, and she closed them, drawing in a deep breath as she forced the memory away. It did no good to journey back through time. She couldn't change the past. She had to concentrate on the present and the future.

She strolled over to where Angel and Damien sat and asked, "May I help build your sand castle?"

"Sure," Angel answered. "We're going to build the biggest one ever, aren't we, Damien?"

"Yes," Damien responded. "Do you know how to build towers, Jenny?"

"Sure do. We need to find something to mold them." She glanced around until she spied an empty soda can that someone preceding the group had discarded on the beach. She retrieved it, carried it back to the food supplies Trevor had provided and dug through them until she found a can opener. She removed one end and carried the can back to Damien. After instructing him on how to build his towers, she began to help build the walls.

The three of them worked together quietly, with Jennifer keeping a careful watch on Damien. He was more relaxed right now than she'd ever seen him, and she had a premonition that something significant was going to happen. Nearly an hour had passed when it finally did.

He was working on the highest wall and grumbling because he was having difficulty. Suddenly he rose to his knees so he could have better access to the area. Angel gasped, and Jennifer barely managed to clap her hand over the girl's mouth to stop her words.

Angel's dark eyes turned on Jennifer in confusion, and Jennifer shook her head and whispered, "Don't say anything to him, honey. I'll explain why later, but don't say anything, okay?"

It was apparent that Angel was still confused, but she nodded, and Jennifer removed her hand and went back to work. Several minutes passed before Damien's eyes suddenly widened with the realization that he was on his knees, and he immediately sat back down, glancing suspiciously toward Angel and Jennifer.

When they both pretended to be unaware of what had occurred, he released a relieved sigh and said, "I'm tired, Jenny. I want my wheelchair."

Jennifer nodded. "All right, Damien. Angel, would you go get his wheelchair for him?"

"But—" the girl began to protest. She stopped when Jennifer shot her a warning look. "I'll get the chair."

"Thank you, Angel," Jennifer said.

The girl returned with the chair and helped Damien into it. Then she wheeled him back to Theresa's side as he requested. She once again returned and sat down beside Jennifer.

"Why didn't we tell him he was on his knees?" she asked without preamble. "I don't think he knew he was."

"He didn't," Jennifer answered. "You see, Angel, Damien really believes that he can't walk, and he's convinced his mind that he can't. Sometimes he forgets to remind his mind that he can't move his legs, and he does something like get up on his knees. If we told him what he was doing, then he'd make an extra effort to make sure his mind doesn't let him do that again. If we don't say anything, then he'll think his secret is safe and he'll let his mind forget again.''

''But if he can get up on his knees, can't he walk?''

''Well, his muscles are stronger now because of his exercises, and he might be able to, but he wouldn't be able to just take off like you and I. He'd have to take it slowly and sort of teach himself how to walk again.''

''I'm confused,'' Angel said with a sigh. ''Doesn't he want to walk, Jenny?''

''Deep down he does, Angel, but he feels very guilty, and he's punishing himself.''

''What did he do that was so bad he wouldn't want to walk?''

Jennifer released her breath slowly. It wasn't her practice to discuss her charges with the others; she gave them only enough information to ensure that inadvertent comments wouldn't cause a crisis. But in Angel's case, it might help her if she had a better understanding of Damien's problems.

''Let's go for a walk,'' Jennifer said, and rose to her feet.

She and the girl strolled along the beach, stopping to investigate a tidal pool as Jennifer told her Damien's story. When she was through, Angel looked up at her with tear-filled eyes that reflected a maturity that should never be seen in a child so young.

''Why does the world have to be so unfair, Jenny?''

''Oh, Angel.'' Jennifer sighed and wrapped her arms around the girl. ''Since time began we've been asking that question, and no one's found the answer yet. Some people seem to go through life with no problems, and others seem to have more than their share. All we can do is try to live the best way we know how and grab on to every little bit of happiness that comes along so we have something to help us through the bad times."

As she spoke, her gaze moved toward the far horizon, and she finally let the coin she'd tossed concerning Trevor fall. He was offering her a chance to grab some happiness, and she wasn't going to let that happiness get away. If an affair was all she could share with him, then that's what she'd share, and she prayed she'd be brave enough to end it before it grew cold and empty.

Trevor dropped wearily down beside Theresa and lifted her hat off her eyes.

"I just wanted to make sure you were still alive," he teased when she winked at him.

"If I look dead to the world, those kids won't try to convince me that I need some exercise. That is one vice I avoid at all costs, as my portly figure proclaims. They worked you out pretty good, didn't they?"

"Killed me is more like it," Trevor answered dryly. "I work out three times a week at the gym, but I think I'm going to have to concentrate on more aerobics."

"Just take about twenty years off your age and you won't have to resort to anything quite so drastic," Theresa said with a laugh. "But if you think they're bad, try keeping up with a two-year-old sometime. I baby-sat my niece for a week last summer, and it almost did me in."

Trevor smiled, remembering. "Damien was like that. He was so active that you had to wear roller skates to keep up with him. Patricia and I would both count down the seconds until it came time for his nap.''

"I'm surprised you didn't hire a nanny to take care of him,'' Theresa stated.

"We'd have missed out on too much fun.''

"But you'd have saved shoe leather.''

"It was worth the price of shoes. Where'd Jenny go?''

"She and Angel walked down the beach. Angel looked upset about something and probably needed to talk.''

"Did Damien do something to her?'' Trevor automatically asked, his brow furrowing as his gaze drifted toward his son, who was looking for seashells with a group of youngsters.

"I don't think so. If something had happened, Damien would be upset, and he isn't.''

Trevor nodded and threaded sand through his fingers.

"Is something on your mind, Trevor?'' Theresa questioned intuitively.

"Get around a couple of female psychologists and a man can't even suffer in peace.'' He laughed.

Theresa laughed too. "I think it's a finely honed mother instinct that Jenny and I have developed. We want to stop problems before they have a chance to begin. It saves a lot of emotional wear and tear.''

"Did you know Jenny's husband?''

"Yes.''

"What was he like?''

"Wonderful. I met Tom and Jenny when I was doing my doctoral work. They'd just graduated and were teaching at the university part-time while they were getting Hamilton House started. Tom had bright red hair, laughing green eyes and was one big walking freckle, but he didn't have that infamous redheaded temper. In fact, I think he was born without a temper. When he and Jenny found out I was also interested in runaways, they sort of took me under their wing. I spent so much time at Hamilton House that, when Tom was killed, it was just natural for me to move my bags in and take up residence. I've been there ever since."

"So it was Jenny's husband who got her interested in runaways?" Trevor questioned, curious.

"Oh, on the contrary." Theresa waved an expressive hand in the air. "It was Jenny who got Tom interested. According to Tom, there was a lecture given in class by a supposed expert in the treatment of runaways. As the man expounded behind the podium, for every point he made, Jenny challenged him. Tom said the man got so red in the face, he thought he'd have a stroke. Finally this expert demanded that Jenny either produce evidence for her assertions or sit down and remain quiet. Tom said Jenny calmly walked up to the podium and said, 'I produce myself.'"

"I produce myself?" Trevor repeated.

"Sure. The man was basing his conclusions on statistics and case histories, but he'd done very few interviews with actual runaways. Jenny was basing her conclusions on experience. She told him that if he wanted to have good, conclusive research, he should get out on the streets and that she'd be glad to introduce him to the entire runaway population in Los Angeles County. He took her up on it, and Tom was so intrigued that he volunteered for the project. That's how he and Jenny met."

"Are you saying Jenny was a runaway?"

"You didn't know?" Theresa asked in surprise.

"No, I didn't."

"Gee, I'm surprised she didn't tell you. It's no secret. Even the kids know it. That's why she's so good at what she does. She's been where they're at, and she knows what's going through their minds even before they do."

"I can see where that would give her a great advantage," Trevor said, wondering just what else Dr. Jennifer Anne Hamilton had failed to reveal about herself.

Jennifer and Angel returned to find that Trevor and Theresa had gathered the kids and were preparing supper. She threw herself into the activities, and after all the kids had been fed, she handed Trevor a plate and urged him through the food line.

After he'd filled his plate and settled down away from the group against some boulders, Theresa said, "I think I blew it for you, Jenny."

"Oh?" Jennifer questioned in surprise.

"Trevor started talking to me after you left, and I let it slip that you were a runaway. I didn't know you were keeping it a secret. I'm sorry."

"Oh, great!" Jennifer groaned.

"I really am sorry," Theresa apologized.

"Don't be ridiculous," Jennifer scolded lightly. "It wasn't exactly a secret. I just . . . hadn't gotten around to saying anything. I'll take care of it."

"Next time you're keeping things quiet, how about letting me know?"

"I will, Theresa. And you didn't do anything wrong."

"That's what you said about Damien after he gave you a fat lip."

Jennifer chuckled. "It's not exactly the same thing."

"You're right. It's not the same thing. It's worse."

"Just go eat," Jennifer ordered.

She filled her plate and moved cautiously toward Trevor, wondering what he was thinking.

"Hi. Still mad at me?" she asked as she approached him.

"Sit," he instructed, patting the ground beside him. Obediently she settled next to him. "I wasn't mad at you, Jenny. I was disappointed in you."

"I know, and I'm sorry. Theresa told me that you and she had a talk."

"I'm sorry she did that," he said. "I'd have preferred that you'd come to me on your own."

Jennifer took a bite of her hot dog before saying, "I would have, Trevor."

"If you say so, Jennifer."

"I really would have."

"Then why did you shut me out like that?"

She sighed, took another bite of hot dog and swallowed it before answering. "If I'd said that I'd been a runaway, you wouldn't have been satisfied with that. You'd have asked me why and been opening up an entirely new can of worms."

"And what can of worms is that?"

"See? You're already doing it."

"Does that mean you're not going to answer me?"

"It depends on how hard you want to push."

"Which means?"

"Will you promise to take my answer at face value and leave the subject alone?"

"For how long?"

"Until I feel secure enough to talk to you about it."

"That's a very thought-provoking statement, Jenny."

"I know."

He drew in a deep breath and said, "Try me."

"That's hardly a promise, Trevor."

"I can't give a promise until I know what I'm promising."

"If I say the subject is closed, will you close it?"

He frowned at the setting sun before replying, "I'll try, but I can't promise."

"I guess that's good enough for now. Did you ever wonder why Edward referred you to me?"

"No. He told me you were the best child psychologist he'd ever met. He showed me your record, which is extraordinary, and I knew he was right."

"He didn't send Damien to me because of my work with the kids, Trevor. He sent him to me for a much more personal reason. Damien killed his mother. I killed my father."

Trevor choked on his hot dog and glanced toward her in disbelief. "Would you repeat that?" he asked when he finally dislodged the food from his throat.

"You heard me the first time."

"But your father was killed in a boating accident! The Coast Guard report said..."

"You did your homework," she stated suspiciously as his voice trailed off.

He flushed guiltily and glanced away from her. "Damien's my son, Jennifer. I had to know who was working with him, and you must admit that your address is a little...questionable."

"Of course," she said stiffly. "What did you do, Trevor? Pick up the telephone and call a private detective?"

"It wasn't a private detective, Jennifer. It was the head of security at Hawke International," he answered, his cheeks a guilty crimson.

At first she was numb as she listened to his confession. But the numbness quickly faded, replaced by an explosion of temper unlike any she'd ever experienced before. "How could you?" she exclaimed angrily.

"Jennifer—"

"Jennifer, nothing!" she interrupted in a soft, deadly whisper. "One of the finest psychiatrists in the country—not to mention that he's your friend—gives you my name, and you have the audacity to have me checked out?"

"Old habits die hard, Jenny, and I am my father's son."

"That's a poor excuse, and you know it! What gave you the right to invade my privacy and then have the gall to ask me to help you and your son?"

"Jenny, you're making a mountain out of a molehill."

"You're just full of little sayings today, aren't you, Trevor?" she questioned sarcastically, her hazel eyes flashing. The rage in them made him grimace and glance away from her as she said, "You want me to confess my innermost secrets to you after you've already hired someone to do it for me. Well, I can tell you right now that you didn't get the full story, because money talks, and when it does, everyone listens. The details of my father's death and my two years as a runaway never went on record because my mother made sure they never did, and as far as I'm concerned, you'll never know them!''

"Jenny!" he exclaimed impatiently, but she rose, threw her plate to the ground and stalked off.

"Some days it just doesn't pay to get up," he muttered to himself, dropping his own plate.

Jennifer walked to the food and started packing it. Someone moved to her side and began to help. She glanced up and discovered the someone was Racer, an orphan who'd been tossed from one foster home to another until he'd finally had enough and decided to go out on his own. He'd been at Hamilton House the longest. He was intelligent, a born leader and was blessed with an insight into people that rivaled Jennifer's own talents. He'd soon be leaving Hamilton House, and Jennifer knew that when he did, she'd sit down and cry like any mother whose child was leaving the nest.

"You're mad," he said quietly.

"I am not mad," she denied. "I'm furious."

"Ain't love great?" He chuckled.

"Love, hell!" she exclaimed.

"Jenny! You said a four-letter word!"

"Actually, I said two of them."

"Yeah, I guess *love* is four letters."

"You're too young for this conversation."

"I'm graduating in May, Jenny."

"You're still too young."

"He's a nice guy, Jenny."

"Nice—heck!"

"See? You're using those four-letter words again."

"He had me investigated!"

Racer's mouth gaped. "Gosh, did he find out anything juicy?"

"No."

"Then why are you so mad?"

"How would you like it if he'd had you investigated?"

"I'm too young for this conversation."

"You're also becoming obnoxious in your old age."

"Oh, I love you." He laughed, grabbed her and gave her a big hug. "Aren't you going to smile for me?"

"Don't press your luck, Racer."

"The name is really Homer," he whispered.

"Yeah, I know, and if you keep being obnoxious, I'm going to tell everyone."

"You wouldn't!"

"No, I wouldn't."

"If it's any consolation, he looks like a thundercloud who lost his lightning."

"He'll find it. And I hope it strikes him where it hurts the most."

"Dr. Hamilton, I'm surprised at you!"

"You're getting too big for your britches, Racer."

"It's called street savvy, Jenny, and you know it."

"Why are we having this conversation?"

"Because I'm the oldest at Hamilton House, and that sort of makes me the man of the house. You're upset, and I want to help."

"You can help the most by not helping. Get my drift?"

"As in wood? Get it? Drift . . . wood?"

"I get it, Ho . . . mer."

"You really want to die young, don't you, Jenny?"

When Jennifer yelled, "All aboard!" no one was brave enough to ignore her. Even Theresa scurried onto the bus, shooting a glare at Trevor on the way. Jennifer was one of the most even-tempered people the entire group had ever met, and he was the recipient of many a scowl as he dropped into the seat behind the bus driver.

Jennifer took a head count twice before curtly telling the bus driver that he could leave. Damien had settled down with Angel in the back of the bus, and Jennifer sat alone in the front seat across from Trevor, tapping her foot impatiently all the way home. Half the group was asleep by the time they arrived, and she and Theresa shook them awake and herded them toward the front door of Hamilton House. She was just heading up the stairs, when Damien's voice sounded behind her.

"Jenny?" he said, sounding so much like the little boy he was that she immediately glanced down at him.

"What is it, Damien?" she responded patiently. She might be angry at the father, but she wasn't about to take it out on the son.

"I think I got a sunburn."

Jennifer frowned and instantly moved down the stairs. "Where, honey?"

"My back. It hurts."

"Let me look. Oh, Damien!" she gasped when she lifted his shirt. She gently touched the angry red skin. "Go into your room, and I'll get your dad. I'm sure he has something we can put on it."

"Will you put it on, Jenny?"

"Of course, sweetheart. You go on in now, and I'll find your father."

As luck would have it, it was Trevor's turn to be in the shower, and Jennifer leaned against the wall outside the bathroom door and waited for him. When he

walked out wearing nothing but a haphazardly secured towel, she gulped, quickly averted her eyes and
said, "Damien has a sunburn. I think it's close to a
second degree, so the first-aid ointment I have probably isn't strong enough. Have you got something I
can put on it?"

"I thought he had sunscreen on," Trevor said with
a frown.

"I did, too, but whether he did or not, he's burned.
Do you have anything, Trevor?" she asked impatiently, eager to get away from his half-naked body,
which, despite her anger, was affecting her equilib-
rium.

"Of course I do. I'll take care of him."

"He . . . asked me to do it," she said hesitantly.

"Fine," he said curtly. "I'll meet you in his room."

"Fine," she repeated, and walked stiffly down the
hallway.

"It really hurts, Jenny," Damien whispered when
she helped him into the bed and bared his back.

"I know it does, sweetheart, but we'll put something on it that will make it feel better."

"My stomach hurts, too."

Jennifer frowned. "How many hot dogs did you
eat?"

"Two."

Two hot dogs shouldn't have been enough to make
his stomach hurt. She felt his forehead. She instantly
shot up off the bed and went in search of a thermometer. She found one in the downstairs bath and had it
in his mouth when Trevor walked into the room.

"He has a fever?" he asked.

"Uh-huh." She pulled the thermometer out of
Damien's mouth.

"How high?"

"Almost a hundred and one," she answered as she walked toward him and handed him the thermometer.

"Damn!" Trevor swore softly after he'd glanced down at it.

"That's common with a burn like this, isn't it?"

"Yes, but he's allergic to aspirin, and I don't have any acetaminophen with me."

"Trevor," she said in an angry whisper, "why didn't you tell me he was allergic to aspirin?"

"I never thought about it," he replied in an angry whisper of his own.

"Dammit, Trevor," she railed at him in a low voice that Damien couldn't hear. "Theresa and I are responsible for this boy when you're not around. Why didn't you give us a medical history?"

"Why didn't you ask for one?"

"Because you're a doctor, and I had the audacity to assume that you'd tell me something like that! Is there anything else he's allergic to?"

"Tetanus and penicillin," he said sheepishly.

"Great!" Jennifer exclaimed, her temper once again erupting. "Two out of three of those are things he'd commonly be treated with—aspirin for almost anything and tetanus for a wound. Trevor, I'm going to count to one hundred and then pray that I won't strangle you."

"Jennifer, I made a mistake, okay? I'm sorry, but no damage has been done."

"No damage?" she repeated incredulously. "No, there hasn't been any damage done, but that's only by accident!"

He brought his hand up to his forehead and massaged it. "You're right, Jenny, and I'm sorry. I should have given you a medical history, but I honestly didn't think about it. I always assume that if something happens, I'll be called before anything is done to him."

She crossed her arms over her chest and glared at him. "Sure. Unless you're in surgery or with a critically ill patient or any other number of circumstances that make you unavailable during an emergency."

"So what do you want me to do?"

"I want you to carry him up to my room and put him into my bed. At least if he gets sick during the night, I can take care of him in a little bit of comfort."

"If he gets sick and I can't take care of him, I'll take him home to Mrs. Ferguson so you won't have to be bothered," he shot back caustically, even though he knew her words hadn't warranted that kind of response. He was angry at himself, not at her. She was right. He should have told her about Damien's allergies, but for some reason, he just hadn't thought about it.

"The hell you will!" she exclaimed angrily. "I took on the responsibility of that boy, and I'm not going to shove him off onto someone else because he gets sick and you decide to play high and mighty! Now just carry him up to my room and put him into my bed."

"He can sleep with me," Trevor responded stubbornly.

She frowned and drew in a deep breath before stating, "Trevor, you have pushed me to my limit today, and I think if you say one more contrary word, I'm going to brain you. Do as you're told. Then I'll be happy, and you'll be alive. Got it?''

"Got it," he repeated, his lips beginning to twitch.

"This is not funny, Trevor."

"I know it's not."

"So why are you almost grinning?"

"You're just so darn cute when you're mad."

"I'm also as nasty as a bear with a sore paw when I've had a bad night, and this looks like one I may never forget."

"That's one of the things that's so attractive about you, Jennifer. A man always knows where he stands with you."

"Good," she sniffed in exasperation. "That means you know you have to have hip boots to wade through the manure you've piled around yourself today."

"Where are you going?"

"To tell Angel that Damien will be with me and then to take a shower. You can take care of your son until then, can't you?"

"Of course, Jenny," he responded with mock meekness. He barely held back a grin when she glared at him suspiciously.

She informed Angel of the situation, assured the girl Damien would be all right and went to take her shower. By the time she walked into her room, Damien was in her bed and Trevor was applying ointment to his back.

"I want Jenny to fix my back," Damien said childishly the moment he saw her.

Trevor sighed and passed her the ointment. She sat down on the edge of the bed and went to work.

"Can Daddy sleep with us, Jenny?" Damien asked.

Her head automatically snapped toward Trevor. She scowled when she discovered he was grinning from ear to ear.

"No, Damien. I'm sorry, but he can't."

"Why not?"

"Because people who aren't married don't sleep in the same bed."

"Then how come I get to sleep with you?"

"Uh, by people, Damien, I mean grown-up people. Grown-up men and women."

She glanced toward Trevor and wanted to punch him in the nose when she discovered his grin still in place. Why didn't he say something? After all, this was his son, not hers, and he knew as well as she did that this conversation was heading in a dangerous direction.

"That's not true, Jenny," Damien said after several seconds had passed. "My friend Tommy's mom and her boyfriend sleep in the same bed, and they're not married."

Trevor's look said "I'm waiting to see you dig your way out of this one." Well, she would, and then *he'd* be digging his way out.

"Well, Damien, Tommy's mom and her boyfriend are a subject called the birds and the bees. That's a subject you should discuss with your dad, since daddies always tell their sons about the birds and the bees."

"Yeah?" Damien glanced toward his father expectantly.

Trevor cleared his throat uncomfortably and shot Jennifer an irritated look. "It's a subject we'll talk about sometime when we're alone, Damien."

"Why?"

Trevor scowled at Jennifer, and she gave him a serene, if slightly malicious, smile. "Because it's a subject that fathers and sons talk about when they're alone."

"But why?"

"Because that's just the way it is, Damien," he answered impatiently. Jennifer giggled.

"Okay," Damien responded with a resigned sigh.

"It's time you and I got settled down for the night," Jennifer announced, "so kiss your father good night so he can leave."

Trevor bent down, and Damien obediently kissed him. Then Jennifer followed him to the door. He stepped out into the hallway and said, "I'm going to go out and get him some Tylenol, Jenny. I'll bring it in as soon as I get back, and if he feels any worse during the night, come wake me. I'll take care of him. You shouldn't suffer because of my irresponsibility. I should have made sure he didn't get too much sun today."

He looked so penitent as he looked at her with those big violet eyes that she sighed, leaned against the doorframe and shook her head in defeat. She couldn't have stayed mad at him if she'd tried.

"I think we were all a little irresponsible today. We all should have kept a better watch on him and made him keep his shirt on most of the time."

"Yeah," he said, stuffing his hands into the pockets of his jeans. "I'm sorry I didn't give you his medical history, Jenny. The only excuse I have is that everyone at home knows it, and I guess it just didn't register that you wouldn't."

"That's partly my fault, too, Trevor. I should have gone through the standard checklist with Damien just as I do with all the kids, and I didn't."

He nodded, glanced down at his bare feet and then back up at her. "Jenny, about the other...argument we had. All I was trying to do was get a little background on you. Who you were and where you came from. There was no digging into your past."

"Snooping is snooping, Trevor, no matter how little or how much," she responded stiffly, and her lips settled into a grim line that told him his explanation had not been accepted.

"I'll go get the Tylenol," he said in defeat.

"Fine," she responded, and turned and walked back into the room.

It took Trevor half an hour to find an open convenience store. When he returned, he immediately went to Jennifer's room. Her door stood open, and he gazed inside, his lips automatically curving into a tender smile.

Damien was curled up against her with his arm wrapped around her waist and his head resting against her breast. Her own arms were wrapped securely around him in a motherly embrace.

They were both sound asleep, and Trevor crept into the room and felt Damien's forehead. It was still warm, so he went to get a glass of water. When he returned, he managed to get Damien awake enough to take the Tylenol without waking Jennifer. Damien obediently took the tablet and then curled back up in Jennifer's arms.

Trevor shook his head as he crept back out of the room. It seemed a sin for a grown man to be jealous of his own son, but he would have given anything to be in Damien's place at the moment.

He entered the room he shared with Racer and Long John, stripped off his clothes and crawled into bed. He folded his hands beneath his head and stared up at the ceiling, unable to summon sleep. For a day that had started out so marvelously, it had sure ended in disaster.

He shifted uncomfortably as his body immediately responded to the memory of sharing his lovemaking fantasy with Jennifer. He closed his eyes and let himself recall the flame of desire in her hazel ones as he'd gazed down into her face.

He rolled to his stomach and pulled his pillow over his head to muffle a groan. He wanted her so badly that it was eating him alive, but now that she knew he'd had her investigated, he was going to have to use some pretty fast footwork to get back into her good graces. He knew he'd find a way. He just hoped he did it before this fire burning him up inside destroyed him.

Chapter Seven

When Jennifer awoke the next morning, she immediately knew something was wrong. She felt too rested, as if she'd finally had enough sleep for once. She quickly sat up in bed and frowned at the clock, which confirmed her dire suspicion that she'd overslept. She let out a soft curse and leaped out of bed. She was supposed to meet the contractor at the construction site, and if she hurried, she'd just make it.

It wasn't until she was on her feet that she registered that Damien was gone. She brushed the hair from her eyes and flushed as she realized that Trevor must have retrieved him. There was something provocative about his creeping into her room and looking at her while she slept. Then she gave an impatient shrug and headed for the bath. Now was not the time to indulge in fantasies.

She performed her morning toilette in record time, pulled on her clothes and raced down the stairs. Theresa was in her favorite spot in the house: in front of the kitchen stove, baking cookies.

"I overslept!" Jennifer gasped as she ran in, grabbed an apple and stuck it into her purse. "If I drive five miles over the speed limit, I might make it to the construction site on time."

"Oh, Jenny, I'm sorry," Theresa apologized sincerely. "If I'd known you had an appointment, I'd never have let Trevor turn off your alarm."

"Trevor turned off my alarm? I'll kill him!"

"He only did it because you looked exhausted, and I agreed with him," Theresa responded with a motherly frown. "You push yourself too hard, Jenny. I tell you that all the time, but you never listen. If you're mad at him, then you have to be mad at me. I conspired with him."

"So I'll kill you both," she grumbled, and Theresa smiled. "I don't know how long this meeting will take," Jennifer continued, "so I don't know when I'll be back. Hold down the fort, okay?"

"Sure."

"By the way, how's Damien this morning?" she asked as she reached the kitchen doorway and glanced over her shoulder.

"He looks a little like an overdone lobster, but he's fine," Theresa answered. "I really felt bad. I should have realized he needed to wear his shirt."

"Well, feel bad with the rest of the grown-ups," Jennifer said wryly. "I didn't think about it, and neither did Trevor. I really do have to run," she said as she glanced at her watch.

Tearing out the front door, she ran full force into a wide, immovable chest.

"Whoa!" Trevor laughed as he caught her. "Is the place on fire?"

"I have a bone to pick with you about tampering with my alarm clock, but I don't have time now," she told him, and gave an admonishing shake of her finger. "I have to make a two-hour drive in less than two hours."

"Where are you going?"

"To the construction site. Now I really do have to run."

"Can I go?"

"You?"

"Why not? Unless you're going up there to have a torrid affair, of course. In that case, I'd be in the way."

"Could we take your car?" she asked with interest.

He chuckled and shook his head. "Jennifer, if I didn't know better, I'd think you only want me for my wheels."

"I do," she responded loftily. "Your car will go over fifty miles an hour and survive. Mine may have to be put to sleep on the side of some strange road."

"Well, I couldn't stand by and let some poor car go to its heavenly reward on the side of a strange road. Let's go."

He helped her into the car, rounded the hood and climbed in beside her. She told him which highway to take, and he headed the car in that direction.

Neither of them spoke until they were on the highway. Then Jennifer broke the silence. "Don't ever turn off my alarm again, Trevor. I know it was a well-meaning gesture, but it could have caused problems.

The contractor is making a special trip to the site—on Sunday, no less—and he would have been quite put out with me if I hadn't shown up.''

"I'm sorry, Jennifer. You just looked beat, and I thought you could use a little extra sleep.''

"Thanks for the thought, but next time resist the urge. Theresa said Damien's all right this morning.''

"He's a little sore, but he'll survive. By the way, that envelope next to you is yours.''

"It is?'' she said, lifting the envelope. "What is it?''

"It's the background report I got on you. I thought you might want to see it.''

She dropped the envelope as if it had burned her and stared at it in disgust. The fact that it contained a report on her made her feel violated.

She glanced out the window. "Thanks, but no thanks. I know everything I need to know about myself.''

"Jennifer, I would appreciate it if you'd look at the report.''

"Why?'' she asked, her temper beginning to flare.

"Because you're angry at me about it, and I want you to see what you're angry about.''

"Are you saying my anger isn't justified?''

"No, Jennifer, I'm not,'' he responded, turning steady violet eyes in her direction. "I realize I wouldn't have liked it if you'd done something like that to me. In my defense, however, I was only doing it out of concern for Damien.''

"Trevor, I think you're missing the whole point here,'' she said with a frown. "What I'm really angry about is that you did this *after* Edward referred you to me. The man is impeccable, and you know it. You were insulting his friendship, and as far as I'm concerned, good friends are too hard to find."

His cheeks reddened in anger, and he shot her an impatient glare. "Jennifer, even Edward is human and capable of making an error in judgment. I basically agree with what you're saying, but I've been used too many times in my life, and there's no way in hell that I will ever put myself into a position where my son can be used as a pawn. You are also blowing this way out of proportion. If you'd look at the report, you'd realize that."

She stared at the vile envelope and shuddered. "I don't want to look at it."

"Then please do it for me, Jennifer."

She glanced up and frowned when those big violet eyes stared at her pleadingly. "All right," she said with a grudging sigh.

She lifted the envelope and pulled out a sheaf of papers. The top sheet gave a list of vital statistics: where she'd been born, who her parents were, where she'd gone to school and the fact that she was widowed. Accompanying that was a copy of the Coast Guard report regarding her father's death, a verification of her state licensure and a letter from her insurance company stating that she had no malpractice suits pending against her.

"This is it?" she said.

"That's it. As you can see, we didn't go into any great depth. I asked for a background check, and that's what I got."

"But if something suspicious had shown up, you would have done more digging."

"And in my place you wouldn't have?" he growled. "Come on, Jennifer, you're behaving very immaturely over this. I offended you, and I'm sorry. Can't we just leave it at that?''

"Why did you need the Coast Guard report?"

He flushed. "Actually, I asked for that. I vaguely remembered the accident and was curious.''

"Curious," she repeated with a brittle laugh. She stuffed the papers back into the envelope and threw it into the back seat so she wouldn't have to look at it again. Then she leaned her head wearily against the seat and closed her eyes.

"You know, Trevor, if I'd ever wondered if I'd done the right thing by leaving the lap of wealth and luxury, you just proved to me that I did. I couldn't live with myself if I had to feel that every person I came into contact with should be investigated because they might want something from me.''

"And you think I enjoy living that way?" he countered. "I hate it, Jennifer, but I have to be concerned about Damien. Especially now that his mother's gone and isn't around to help keep an eye on things. It won't be too much longer before people begin to use him. I remember too clearly what that was like, and it makes me ill when I realize he's going to have to go through it. I'm just doing my part to stop that from happening as long as possible.''

She turned her head and gazed at him solicitously. "At least you realize you can't protect him forever. But you're shortchanging yourself in the meantime. I've been used, too, Trevor, and you know as well as I do that after a while you develop a sort of sixth sense. You instinctively know when you come up against someone you can't trust. Start trusting that sixth sense a little more and your father's security chief a little less, and you'll be a lot happier.''

"When does your book of philosophy go on sale?" he asked, glancing toward her with a teasing grin.

"As soon as I learn how to type. Since I'm all thumbs, that may be a long-time. You have to take the next exit."

"So am I forgiven?" he asked as he took the exit.

"I suppose so. You're too pitiful not to forgive."

"Thanks a lot," he said dryly.

"You're welcome," she answered.

"So tell me what I'm going to see at this construction site of yours."

"Some big holes and a few sticks of wood."

"No wonder you're meeting with your contractor. Having problems?"

"Only ones of my own making. Every time the architect gets the plans drawn up, I turn around and think of something else I want to add. The last time I met with Ron—that's the contractor, by the way—he grumbled something about women not knowing their own minds. I don't think he's too happy with me."

"You don't seem too concerned about it."

"The more I change, the more his estimate goes up. He'll survive."

"Sounds reasonable to me. How about doing me a favor?"

"What's that?"

"Scoot over here next to me. I'm still feeling wounded and need some reassurance."

She couldn't help the smile that curved her lips. "I don't know. It looks to me like you've licked your wounds pretty well."

"On the outside I'm smiling. On the inside I'm crying."

"And you expect me to buy that?"

"Yes."

"Haven't you ever been to one of those driver's safety lectures where they tell you that boys and girls shouldn't sit next to each other in the car? It interrupts your concentration and makes you more prone to accidents."

"Jennifer, would you just scoot over here? I promise I'll keep my eyes on the road."

"Well, I guess if you promise," she drawled, and scooted over.

Her blood pressure skyrocketed when he put his hand on her thigh and gave it a squeeze. Things were getting pretty bad if all he had to do was touch her to send her into orbit.

"I have a confession to make," he said.

"Another one? Don't you want to let your wounds heal before you get another tongue-lashing?"

"This has to do with my current wounds."

"Oh? So tell me this confession."

"Last night I was jealous of my son."

"Jealous?" she repeated in disbelief. "You're kidding me. Why were you jealous?"

"Because he got to lie in your arms all night. I hated it. I wanted it to be me."

"That sounds serious, Trevor. Rivalry between father and son is definitely not good," she said with a chuckle. "What makes it even worse is you were jealous of a little boy who wasn't feeling good and needed a woman's touch."

"I haven't been feeling too good myself lately, and I definitely need a woman's touch," he responded, rubbing his hand sensuously along her thigh.

"Is that right?" she asked, making a halfhearted effort to catch his hand. He easily eluded her. "Just where do you need this, uh, woman's touch?"

He chuckled. "If you don't know that, Jennifer, I think you need to sit in on my birds-and-bees talk with Damien. By the way, that was a dirty trick."

"You saw where the conversation was leading, and you didn't do anything to help stop it," she responded airily. "You got just what you deserved. Besides, he's old enough to know the facts of life. Trevor, stop it!" she finished impatiently when his hand began to stray provocatively. She made a wholehearted effort to catch his hand this time, but he still managed to elude her.

"Why? I have my eyes on the road. You're not driving, so it's okay for you to be all hot and bothered."

"Trevor," she stated in a tone that brooked no argument, "you are to stop it right now."

"Okay." He sighed and slid his hand down to her knee. "But you're endangering Damien's sex education."

"And just how am I doing that?"

He shot her a grin. "I've been a widower for a long time, Jennifer. I need to refamiliarize myself with the equipment."

She laughed uproariously and shook her head. "If you ever lose your fortune, Trevor, don't try to take up a career as a con man. You're too transparent."

"I love it when you laugh," he said, his eyes moving over her face in a tender caress. "It lights up your whole face. Will you teach me how to laugh and be happy like you, Jenny? I can't remember ever being really, really happy.''

"Oh, Trevor," she said as tears filled her eyes. She reached up to touch his cheek.

"Hey," he said gruffly as he caught her hand and brought it to his lips. "You're supposed to teach me how to be happy, not how to cry."

"Maybe you need to learn both," she said quietly. "Part of the secret of being happy is to let your emotions run their full gamut."

"Then teach me both," he replied as he wrapped his arm around her shoulder and pulled her against his side.

She rested her head on his shoulder and her hand on his thigh. She was afraid to really analyze the words he'd spoken. They'd touched a chord deep inside that had never been touched before, and she knew if she explored it she'd be straying into dangerous territory. So she just closed her eyes and let herself enjoy being close to him, silently admitting that her heart had taken one more step toward falling irrevocably in love.

They completed the remainder of their journey in companionable silence. When they finally arrived, Jennifer grimaced. The contractor was leaning against his truck and eyeing his watch with a scowl.

"I think you might need to get the whip and chair out of the truck," she said to Trevor as she scooted across the seat and jumped out of the car, prepared to face the lion. "I'm sorry I'm late, Ron," she called out as she began running toward him. "I overslept this morning."

"Would have liked to have done that myself," the man muttered disgruntledly as he watched Trevor approach.

"This is Trevor, Ron," Jennifer said. "Trevor, this is Ron."

The two men exchanged handshakes before Ron turned his attention back to Jennifer. "In order to add that wing you want, we'll have to do a lot more digging," he said, walking toward the cavernous holes for the foundation of Hamilton House.

Jennifer fell into step beside him. "I understand that, Ron."

"You also realize that we're now going to be digging up the basketball court, don't you?"

"We'll relocate the basketball court."

"You've expanded to a size that will require an additional water heater and another furnace."

"Adam explained that when he drew up the new plans."

The man came to a stop beside the holes, gazed down into them and then glanced over at Jennifer. "Look, Jennifer, I'm going to be blunt with you. You're driving me crazy. You want this project done by the end of the year, and at this rate, I won't even have the foundation poured by then. Not only that, you're wasting money. Every time I have to bring in the big machines to dig an additional hole, you get charged for the time it takes them to drive the equipment in and drive it back out. I want you to promise me that before I bring them back, this is the last hole. If you can't promise that, then I'm waiting until you can."

"This is the last hole, Ron."

"You're sure?" he asked doubtfully.

"After that threat I have to be."

He suddenly grinned and shook his head. "I just hate to see you lose money that could be used for the kids you're building this place for."

"I know, and you're right. This is it. No more holes. I promise."

"Fine. Let's go back to my truck. I've got some samples of things you should look at, and I need you to make a few decisions before I start scheduling some of the subcontractor work. Since we'll start pouring the foundation next week, I'm going to have to get things rolling."

He shot her a doubtful look when he talked about pouring the foundation, and she resisted the urge to grin. She glanced back over her shoulder and saw Trevor staring down into the holes, an odd expression on his face. She wondered what he was thinking, but they'd reached the truck and Ron was already hauling out a list of items and samples she needed to take care of. A minute later, she'd all but forgotten about Trevor.

Trevor stood for a long time staring down into the holes and then shoved his hands into his pockets. He turned to look at Jennifer. Until he'd seen the holes, it hadn't really registered that she'd be moving up here. She'd told him, and he'd listened, but it had just never registered. Suddenly he felt ill, and he walked away, moving toward a stand of trees in the distance.

There was a whirring sound overhead. He stopped and raised his eyes to gaze at a biplane as it circled above him and then flew off. When it was gone, he resumed his walk. A smile touched his lips as he watched a huge robin fly from a corner tree. It reminded him of the night Jenny had comforted Damien after his nightmare. When the robin flew behind the trees, Trevor had the urge to race to see where the bird had gone, and before he even knew what was happening, he was running. Then he was passing the trees, and he burst into a beautiful meadow. He stopped short and blinked in surprise to see the robin sitting in the middle of the meadow, catching a worm.

With a feeling of déjà vu, his eyes sought out the tallest tree, and he watched the robin fly to a nest there.

"I don't believe this," he muttered, and ran his hand through his hair. "It's spooky."

"You found Love's Magic Meadow," Jennifer suddenly said behind him, and he spun around to face her. "Sorry, I didn't mean to startle you," she apologized when she saw the look on his face.

"You told Damien about this."

She looked surprised. "Yes. I didn't know he'd told you."

"He didn't. I woke up that night and knew something was wrong. When I came down to check on him, you were already there. I didn't want to interrupt, so I waited at the door in case you needed me."

"Hmm." She stepped to his side. "This is my favorite place in all the world. No matter how bad things get, I can close my eyes and come here. Pretty soon I'll be able to walk up a path and have it for real."

"It's a very beautiful place," he admitted. "Is that why you bought this land?"

"Yes. I first found the meadow when I was fourteen. I was filled with guilt over my father's death and had put my mother through six months of living hell. I couldn't deal with my problems, so I ran away from home. Three days later, scared and lonely, I ended up here. From the moment I walked into the meadow, I felt . . . *loved* is the only word I can use to describe my feelings. I spent a week here and then moved on.''

A wistful smile curved her lips. ''During the next two years, I wandered from one coast to the other and back. The memory of this meadow helped me survive those two years. When I returned to California, I came here, certain it had all changed and that I'd be disappointed. To my surprise, it was exactly the same. I spent another week here and then went home to a very worried and distraught mother, who grabbed me and hugged me and then started a lecture that's still going on.''

''You spent *two years* on the streets?'' Trevor asked in disbelief. ''How did you survive?''

''Sometimes I'm not certain I did,'' she stated with a thoughtful frown. ''I saw and lived through a lot of things that made me grow up fast. After those two years I decided to become a psychologist and work with runaways. I started back to school, worked very hard to make up the lost years of education and entered college right on schedule. I met Tom while I was working on my Ph.D., and lucky for me, he shared my dream. We opened Hamilton House.

''Then, after he died, I was in so much pain that I came to the one place I knew could make me better. To my surprise, the land was up for sale, and I bought it. I'd planned all along to eventually move Hamilton House to the country. I wanted to get the kids away from the city and out into the wide-open spaces. But I was so busy that I'd never gotten around to looking for land, and I think it was because I was fated to end up here.''

"And your current site becomes a temporary refuge? How is that going to work, Jennifer?"

She shrugged. "Kids looking for help will find it. Those who can't be sent back to their families will be sent to me here."

"And who's going to be running this refuge house?"

"I'm not certain yet. The mayor would like to see the city take it over, but there are budget constraints. If they can't handle it, then I will."

"And where will you find the money?"

"I'll find it, Trevor."

She sat down on the ground and reverently touched the petals of a single orange flower. Trevor watched her and knew he'd never felt more removed from her than he did at this very moment. The sun glinted across her auburn hair, and her hazel eyes reflected the verdant field that surrounded her. A sudden bolt of fear ripped through him. She looked so ethereal, so much a part of this place, that he felt if he reached out to touch her, she'd disappear. That all of it would disappear, and he'd be left standing here with nothing.

He turned away from her and stared across the meadow, his eyes filled with unshed tears. He suddenly knew that he was in love with her and he'd already lost her. This was her place—her land—and she belonged here. He'd never be able to take it away from her or her away from it.

As if sensing his distress, Jennifer appeared at his side and asked, "What is it, Trevor?"

He smiled down at her, making no attempt to hide his tears. "Nothing. You just looked so lovely sitting there, Jenny. I suppose you touched my artist's soul."

"That's very poetic," she stated quietly. "Very beautiful."

"Whenever you're around me, all I see is beauty," he replied as he grabbed her and pulled her into his arms, hugging her to him desperately.

"Hey!" She laughed. "If you keep squeezing me like this, all you're going to see is flat!"

"Sorry." He relaxed his hold. "All done with Ron?"

"Yeah. I think he's decided to like me despite his better judgment."

"I don't blame him. You have to like someone as pitiful as you."

"Thanks a lot! Since when have I been pitiful?"

"Since I discovered that you can't make a decision on how many holes to dig. You must have had some traumatic experience back in your sandbox days that warped this side of your personality."

"It's probably the fact that I never had a sandbox so I never got to dig my quota of holes," she said with a giggle.

"That must be it. And poor Ron is paying for it. So, what should we do with the rest of the day?"

"Well, we really should get back to Hamilton House," she replied reluctantly. "Leaving Theresa alone with twenty-one charges is what I'd call cruel and unusual punishment."

He brushed the hair that a breeze had blown into her face away from her eyes. "I was hoping you'd give me a little time, Jenny. We're never alone, and I'd like to be alone with you."

"We're alone now."

"I know, but I'd like to... get away from here."

"Why?"

He shrugged, unwilling to admit that this land of hers made him feel like an intruder. "Wandering feet, I guess. Will you give me a few hours?"

"Yes," she answered, resisting the urge to say she'd give him a lifetime. Because she suddenly realized that she'd like to do just that. But lifetimes weren't meant for two dedicated professionals traveling separate career paths. Only moments were, and she wanted as many moments as she could get from him.

"Great. Let's drive for a while and see what other sights are around here."

"I have a feeling you're going to be disappointed, Trevor. Tourism is not the biggest business in this area."

"We'll find something to entertain us," he said suggestively, and he grabbed her around the waist and spun her in a circle. She was laughing wildly when he brought them to a stop, nuzzled her ear and whispered, "Race you to the car."

"I don't know," she said with a sigh, nuzzling him back. "You'd probably cheat."

"I wouldn't cheat!" he exclaimed in mock offense.

"Good, because I would," she said, and took off on a run.

"Imp!" he yelled as he took off after her.

He passed her halfway to the car and was leaning against it, blowing on his nails and polishing them on his shirt, when she arrived, gasping for breath.

"You, Jennifer, are definitely out of shape," he stated smugly.

"That's what I love, a humble winner," she said and collapsed against him, breathing in the scent of him and reveling in it. "You didn't even work up a sweat."

"I guess I'm too rich to sweat." He chuckled and rubbed her back. "Take slow, deep breaths, Jenny, and you'll be okay."

"Have that engraved on my tombstone, all right?"

"Sure." He laughed. "Oh, God, I love the feel of you," he murmured as he hugged her close to him.

"So you'll keep me around even if I am out of shape?" she asked as she snuggled against his chest.

"You bet. How about if we stop in that little one-horse town down the road and call Theresa? You can tell her we'll be gone for a while and make sure everything's all right."

"That's very thoughtful, Trevor."

"No, it's not," he said, and tilted her head up. After he'd stolen a quick kiss, he said, "It's selfish. I want you to be relaxed and enjoy yourself with me, and you won't do either if your mind is on Hamilton House."

"I think, Dr. Hawke, that you are beginning to know me too well."

"Good. Let's go call Theresa."

He opened the door on the driver's side, and Jennifer scooted in ahead of him. They drove to the small town down the road, and while Jennifer called Theresa, Trevor wandered into an old-fashioned soda fountain. Jennifer was just hanging up when he walked back out and stuck a triple-decker ice-cream cone into her hand.

"All for me?" she teased as she accepted the towering cone.

"Nope. You have to share."

"What if I don't want to share?"

"I'll steal a bite anyway. Hop into the car."

"Where are we going?"

"To do something I haven't done since I was eighteen years old."

"What's that?"

"Just get in the car and you'll find out."

"Where are we going?" she asked again when he climbed in beside her.

"You'll see."

"Trevor, I can't stand the suspense. Tell me."

"Nope. Let me have a lick," he ordered as he watched her eat the cone.

"Not until you tell me where we're going."

"Wanna bet?" He laughed, grabbed her hand and licked the cone.

Their eyes met and locked as he took another lick, letting his tongue ease toward the top and then circle it. There was something very erotic about the action, and she gulped and squirmed uncomfortably on the seat.

His eyes were dark with desire, and she trembled when he smiled and said, "Lick the cone, Jenny."

"I already have."

"Do it again."

He was easing the cone toward her lips, and she obediently licked the ice cream, her pulse beginning to pound as his eyes flared brightly as he watched her.

"Again," he whispered.

"Trevor, you're making me—"

"Lick it again, Jenny," he interrupted huskily.

"Trevor, eating ice cream is not supposed to be...sexy."

"Lick the cone, Jenny."

"Don't look at me and I will."

"Lick the cone, Jenny."

She gave in and licked again. Suddenly he groaned, grabbed her head and pulled her mouth to his. His tongue pushed insistently against her lips. She finally parted them, and his tongue stole inside to explore her every hidden secret until she felt ravished.

She was breathing shallowly and her cheeks were flushed when he finally pulled away.

"The cone's dripping," he said, and licked the melted ice cream off her hand.

"Trevor, what are you trying to do to me?"

"Make you want me as much as I want you," he answered, and licked the cone again.

She closed her eyes tightly and drew in a deep breath, but it did nothing to cool the flames of desire that had unfurled deep within her and were spreading at an alarming rate.

Her eyes snapped open when he suddenly started the car and eased it away from the curb. She cast him a surreptitious glance and took a lick of the cone, which was now beginning to melt quite rapidly. And no wonder. The heat radiating from her body would probably melt down a nuclear core.

They rode in silence, sharing the cone until it was gone, and Jennifer frowned when, several miles out of town, Trevor turned onto an unpaved side road that looked as if it went nowhere.

"Trevor, where are we going?" she once again asked.

"You'll see. We're almost there."

She frowned again when he pulled off the road into a grove of trees, switched off the ignition and turned to face her.

"We're here?" she asked in confusion.

"We're here."

She glanced around the grove of trees and shook her head. "What are we doing here?"

"I told you. We're going to do something I haven't done since I was eighteen."

"What's that?"

"Park and neck."

She blinked at him in disbelief. "In broad daylight?"

"Why not?"

"In the front seat or the back?" she asked, curious.

He gave her a devilish grin. "We could try both, but I think the back would be more fun."

"You're really serious about this, aren't you?"

"I sure am."

"Trevor, this is ridiculous!"

"Why?"

"Well, because it is."

"When was the last time you made love in a car?"

"Now I know you're crazy!" she exclaimed. "You don't really expect us to...in the car in broad daylight?" she asked as she stared at him, wide-eyed.

"Let's just see what happens," he drawled huskily. He caught her head and once again brought her lips to his.

His kiss was urgent, demanding, and with a groan she wrapped her arms around his neck and arched toward him, losing herself so completely that she was scarcely aware when he opened the door, lifted her out and put her into the back seat without ever losing his hold on her lips.

"Jenny, this is ridiculous!" he groaned much later, resting a heated cheek against her exposed breast.

"It is?"

"Yes, it is, and you know it," he grumbled. "There's no way we can make love back here!"

"Didn't you do it when you were eighteen?"

"Smart aleck."

His tongue began stroking a rosy nipple. When he drew it into his mouth, Jennifer let out a sigh of exquisite pleasure and tangled her fingers in his hair, urging him closer. A few minutes later, he released her nipple and rubbed his cheek against the hard nub like a contented cat. "Jenny, my leg is going to sleep. Why don't we leave here and go to my house?"

"Absolutely not!" she exclaimed, even as her body arched toward him hungrily. "This is just perfect. Oh, Trevor," she sighed wantonly when his fingers began to toy with her breast. He lowered his head so his lips could mimic the action at her other breast.

"Let's go back to Hamilton House," he gasped when her hips rotated beneath him urgently.

"Fine, but we can't make love there."

"Why not?"

"Because it's against everything I teach about the chickens and the frogs."

"I'm ordering fried chicken and frog legs for dinner every night this week," he muttered. "Oh! My leg!" he suddenly groaned, shifting so that Jennifer was half sitting and half reclining on the seat.

"Is it asleep?" She giggled when he began to rub it.

"I think it died."

"Poor Trevor," she commiserated, giggling again.

"You're a cruel woman, Jennifer."

"I know."

"I suppose a motel is out." He sighed disgruntledly as he sat up and pulled her onto his lap.

"Definitely," she agreed breathlessly when his hands began to move over her insistently. "Hey, that tickles!" she protested a moment later, and slapped his hand when he devilishly tickled her again.

"Why's a motel out?"

She grimaced. "Too sordid. I'd feel like the proverbial Mr. and Mrs. John Smith."

"We could register as Ms. Jane Doe and friend," he offered helpfully.

"You're insane!" she accused with a laugh.

"Turned on, too," he whispered before dropping several passionate and totally shattering kisses to her lips. He eased her back on his arm and parted her blouse so his eyes could drift over the treasures he'd discovered. "I have to make love to you, Jenny."

"You will."

"When?"

"When all the logistics are right."

"And when will that be?" He was beginning to get irritable.

"Soon," she soothed.

"How soon, Jennifer?" he demanded, shifting again so that she was beneath him, and he urgently eased his hips against her.

Despite the clothing separating them, she could feel the strength of his arousal pressed insistently against her abdomen, and she had to struggle to find her voice.

"Friday night," she said.

"That's five days from now, Jenny. I may die by then. Why Friday night?"

"I can arrange for Theresa to have some help. When we do make love, I don't want us to be hurried. I want us to have all night."

His breath came out in a rush, and he sat up and combed his fingers through his hair. "How about all weekend?"

"All weekend?" she repeated uncertainly, sitting up beside him and wrapping her shirt around her.

He nodded. "If you can get help for one night, you can surely get help for two days and two nights."

"I don't know. I suppose I could, but since your partner took your call this weekend, won't you be on call next weekend?"

"I'll get my other partner to take it. He owes me a few weekends. What do you say?"

"If I can swing it, all weekend," she answered.

"Thank God," he groaned, and pulled her into his arms. He crushed her bare breasts against his bare chest and breathed raggedly against her hair. His hands trembled as they explored her every feminine curve. "Where would you like to spend the weekend, since Hamilton House is out?"

"I know a special place where we can go. It's beautiful, it's isolated and it's perfect."

"Just where is this special place?"

"It's a cabin in the woods."

"Really? Who's cabin?"

"Mine. It was my father's."

"It sounds perfect." He sighed, tried to shift her again and then said, "Oh, damn, your blouse is caught in my belt. Help me get it loose."

"Trevor?"

"Uh-huh?" he said as he managed to free her blouse.

She was staring out the back window at the car approaching them. "Is that man behind us with the red light and the gun your friend?'' she asked conversationally.

"What?'' Trevor gasped. He shot up in the seat and cracked his head on the roof. "Ow! Oh, dear God, Jenny, it's a police officer!''

"I know.'' She giggled helplessly. "Did you hurt your head?''

"To hell with my head!'' he railed. "What am I going to tell him?'' He was hurriedly buttoning his shirt.

"That you're a doctor and that you were giving me mouth-to-mouth resuscitation?'' she offered, clutching her sides as she roared with laughter. "He...he might even...believe you if you remember to zip up...your fly!'' she finished on a howl.

"Jennifer Anne Hamilton, you should be put on the rack!'' he exclaimed in exasperation. "This is *not* funny!''

"Sure it is,'' she gasped, trying to control her laughter but failing miserably.

"We'll talk about this when I get back,'' he said ominously. And he tossed open the car door before the police officer had managed to reach them.

Several minutes passed before he climbed into the front seat and rested his head against the steering wheel. "I have never been so humiliated in my life,'' he mumbled. "He gave me a ticket for loitering.''

"Poor Trevor.'' She chuckled as she leaned over the seat and rumpled his hair. "Being eighteen isn't too much fun, is it?''

"Imp.'' He turned and hauled her over the back of the seat so that she tumbled into his arms. "I remember now why I stopped parking and necking.''

"Why?'' she asked, grinning up at him.

"You always go home frustrated."

"Only until Friday," she replied, and sealed her promise with a kiss.

Chapter Eight

Jennifer was up before dawn the next morning. Her tryst in the country with Trevor had put her even further behind schedule. She had four charts that had to be written up and sent to the state Social Services Department before the end of the day. She had to sign the checks for the bills on her desk, and she had to work out a new counseling schedule. Most of the youngsters required no more than weekly person-to-person counseling once they were settled into Hamilton House's routine, but she was going to have to a start a more intensive program for Damien. She'd also received a call from another halfway house with a problem child they wanted her to take over. That meant she'd have to program time for that child as well as buy another bed and try to figure out where to put the girl.

If the new Hamilton House were done, she'd have more than enough room. The new wing she'd decided to add would handle a significant overflow and would be used primarily for those kids she called short-timers—the ones who were only with her a week or two and then went home.

She yawned as she walked from the kitchen toward the front door. Some of the papers she needed were still in the car, and she had to get them before she could finish the chart she was working on. With Damien sleeping in her office, she had to do her early-morning and late-night work in the kitchen, but that didn't bother her. It kept her in proximity to the cof-feepot.

She yawned again, then gasped when she passed the hall closet and the door flew open. An arm wrapped around her waist, pulled her inside and the door closed behind her.

"Hi, gorgeous. Want a kiss?"

"Is this some kind of mugging?" She chuckled.

"Sort of. Are you going to kiss me?"

"I might. What are you doing in the closet?"

"Waiting for a kiss, of course."

"Well, I can't keep a man waiting, can I?"

"You most certainly can't," Trevor growled, and swept her up in his arms. "A man could get used to a morning kiss like that very fast," he rasped when he finally broke away from her lips.

"A woman, too." She sighed and rested her head against his shoulder. Her hand stroked up and down his chest. "I can feel your heart pounding."

"If that's all you can feel, you're still asleep," he said with a chuckle.

"Why are you up so early anyway?"

"Surgery at seven."

"It's going to be another long day, huh?"

"It sure is. I'm going to miss you."

"I'll miss you, too. Want some coffee before you go?"

"No, I'll get some at the hospital. Want to walk me to my car?"

"Sure."

He grabbed her hand, laced his fingers with hers and peeked out of the closet. "All clear. Let's go."

"You're getting pretty good at this," she teased as they tiptoed past her open office and the community room where Damien and Angel slept respectively.

"And they say you can't teach an old dog new tricks." He swung their hands between them as they stepped out the front door and walked toward his car.

"I'd never call you an old dog, Trevor."

"Good." He leaned against the car, pulled her between his thighs and kissed her breathless.

"We shouldn't do this, Trevor."

"Why not?"

"The kids. If they should see us . . ."

"Jennifer, after your lectures on the chickens and the frogs, they know what's happening without seeing it. Believe me."

Her brow furrowed in a worried frown. "Do you really think so?"

"Yes."

"Oh."

"What does 'oh' mean?"

"It means that we have to set a good example. I can't tell them to behave one way and then act another way myself."

"Then set them a good example, Jenny. Show them how wonderful a relationship can and should be. I promise to be on my best behavior around them if you promise not to act as if nothing's going on."

"I don't know," she said, unconvinced.

"Jennifer, these kids are all going to grow up and become involved in affairs of one kind or another. If they see us behaving openly, naturally and lovingly toward each other, then they see the good side of a relationship. If they see us sneaking around and acting like criminals, then they're going to put a different kind of connotation on it. Whatever you present to them is what they'll eventually mimic. Don't you want them to have open relationships?"

"Of course."

"Then behave like Jenny would behave in a good, normal, healthy relationship."

"I suppose you're right."

"I know I am," he said. Reluctantly he eased her away from him. "I'll see you tonight. And don't forget to start lining up some help for the weekend."

"You sound awfully eager."

"I'm counting down the hours. By Friday, I'll be counting down the seconds. Love you," he said, blowing a kiss as he climbed into his car.

"I love you, too," she whispered as she watched him drive away. And suddenly she felt as if the entire weight of the world were resting on her shoulders.

He wanted her to behave the way she'd behave in a good, normal healthy relationship. The problem was, this relationship was not good, not normal and definitely not healthy. What was even worse, she knew she wasn't going to do anything to stop it from progressing further. With a morose sigh, she went to her car and retrieved the papers she needed.

"Good morning, darling!" a cultured voice trilled later that morning.

Jennifer glanced up from her work to smile at her mother, who stood framed in the doorway in her designer jeans and everyday diamonds. She was three inches shorter than Jennifer, and her hair was black, but their features were so closely matched that no one would have doubted their relationship.

"Good morning, Monica. Out slumming?"

Monica chuckled, walked into the office and plopped down in the chair beside Jennifer's desk. "No more than you are when you manage to wander up into my neck of the woods."

"Touché," Jennifer said. "So, to what do I owe the honor of this visit? It isn't a holiday, it isn't my birthday and I haven't offended anyone significant for at least a month."

"You make me sound like an awful mother, Jennifer," Monica admonished with a pout.

"You're not. You're a good mother. So what's up?"

"You tell me," Monica replied, propping a ring-studded hand beneath her chin and arching a brow. "Rumor has it that you have the Hawke son and grandson living under your roof."

"You mean it's taken you this long to find out?"

"Then it's true?"

"It's true."

"How...interesting. Why?"

"Why what?"

"Why are they living here?"

"Would you believe they both ran away from home?"

The impish grin that curved Monica's lips so closely resembled her daughter's that it was eerie. "I'll believe that if you'll believe I drink domestic champagne."

"Okay, you win!" Jennifer laughed. Then her expression sobered. "Edward referred Damien to me."

"I see," Monica stated quietly, and glanced toward the window. "I'd heard about Damien's problems, and I have to say I sympathized with Trevor."

"I have to say I sympathized with you after my first run-in with Damien. I put you through a lot you didn't deserve, and I'm sorry."

"Hey, that was a long time ago," Monica said. She gave Jennifer's hand a fond squeeze. "I got my baby back, and that's all that matters to me."

"Thanks," Jennifer whispered, squeezing her mother's hand in return.

"So what do you think of the dashing Dr. Hawke?" Monica inquired too nonchalantly, and Jennifer burst into laughter again.

"If you're matchmaking, forget it. Trevor and I can handle things on our own."

One of Monica's perfectly plucked brows arched knowingly. "Well, at least I'm glad to hear you have things to handle. You told me how Damien got here. How did Trevor get here?"

Jennifer gave her mother a quick rundown on the story, and Monica shook her head in amusement. "You know, Jennifer, I've heard of many ingenious ways of luring a man into your lair, but this is the best I've heard yet."

"Monica!" Jennifer exclaimed impatiently. "You know me better than that!"

"Unfortunately I do," Monica sighed. "I guess this means I don't have to go out and pick up a wedding dress."

"No, you do not have to pick up a wedding dress."

"You can't blame a mother for hoping, Jennifer."

"I won't blame you."

"Thanks. Well, I do have to run. I just had to stop by and learn the scoop in person. Give Trevor my best, and tell him I'll see him on the social circuit soon."

"I will, Monica. Don't play too hard."

"A person can never play too hard, Jennifer. I wish you'd learn that."

"I'm a hopeless case."

After her mother had gone, Jennifer frowned down at the paperwork on her desk. Her mother's comment about seeing Trevor on the social circuit had hit home with a thud. If ever there were two mismatched people, it was definitely she and Trevor. He lived the life his money and status offered. She lived like Old Mother Hubbard in a shoe with so many children she didn't know what to do. So why was she so attracted to him? Outside of the obvious, of course.

She knew why, naturally. Beneath that handsome exterior, he was kind, sympathetic, and oddly enough, there was a guilelessness to him that touched her heart. Like yesterday, when he'd asked her to teach him how to be happy. There weren't many men who'd openly confess something like that, nor were there many who'd ask for help. There also weren't many who'd move into Hamilton House and fit in as if they belonged. He liked the kids, and they liked him.

She let out another morose sigh and went back to work. She could sit all day and make lists of his attributes or his faults, and it still wouldn't change anything. She was in love with him, and that was that.

Around noon, Theresa stuck her head in the door and announced, "There's a delivery for you, Jenny."

"A delivery? What kind of delivery?"

"Big and bulky, and the man says you have to sign for it personally."

"It looks like a painting," Jennifer stated when she arrived at the front door and looked at the package sitting at the man's feet.

He grinned and said, "That's because it is. Are you Dr. Hamilton?"

"Yes. Who's it from?"

"The man said to tell you he hopes it touches your artist's soul. Mean anything?"

"Yes," Jennifer whispered. She signed for the painting and carried it into her office.

"I bet I know who it's from," Theresa teased.

"I bet you do, too," Jennifer responded. She set the painting on the chair and tore off the paper. Her hands flew to her mouth, and she gasped, "It's beautiful!"

"Boy, you can say that again," Theresa said in awe.

"I knew he was good, but I didn't know he was *this* good!"

"You mean Trevor did this?"

"Yes," Jennifer answered, and gently ran her fingers over the painting. It was a portrait of two lovers shrouded beneath the drooping boughs of a willow tree, sharing an ardent kiss.

There was a note stuck in one corner. Jennifer pulled it off and opened it. It read:

I wanted to give you a special part of me. A part that money can't buy and a part I've never shared with anyone else. Don't slip through my fingers, Jenny. I need you.

Tears welled in her eyes, and she brought the note to her lips. She would slip through his fingers, and he knew it. Just as he would slip through hers. She now realized that the upcoming weekend was wrong. It would be better to call the whole thing off. The more they became involved, the more tangled in the web they'd become, and they'd both end up with broken hearts.

"You're in love with him, aren't you, Jenny?" Theresa questioned solicitously. She wrapped her arm around Jennifer's shoulders when she nodded and swiped at her eyes.

"I shouldn't have let it happen, Theresa. I shouldn't have."

"Why?"

"Because we're moving to the country. That's a two-hour drive from here and even farther from Beverly Hills. We could never have anything permanent. I couldn't give up Hamilton House, and Trevor couldn't give up his practice. It means as much to him as Hamilton House does to me."

"He could commute."

"Almost five hours a day round trip? He couldn't do that, Theresa. Worst of all, I promised to spend this coming weekend with him, and now I can't."

"Why can't you?"

"Because I think he's falling in love with me, too. If I let this go any further, we're both going to end up hurt. And I don't want to see him hurt."

Theresa gave a solemn nod before saying, "Jenny, I'm going to ask you a question, and I want you to answer it honestly, okay?"

"Okay." Jennifer sniffed.

"If you had known that Tom was going to be killed before you married him, would you still have married him?"

"Yes," she answered instantly.

"Why?"

"Because I'd never trade those happy years for anything."

"Don't you think that you and Trevor also deserve some happy times together?" Theresa asked, her dark brown eyes searching Jennifer's face. "You know it's eventually going to end, so grab on to it and love every minute of it. Just like you did with Tom and would have even if you'd known how it would end."

"That sounds like perverse logic, Theresa."

"It's not. Think about it for a while. Remember, Trevor also knows it will have to end, and he seems willing to take that chance. Love should never be wasted, Jenny. It's a very special gift that should be savored for as long as you can hold on to it."

"Now where in the world did you ever come up with something like that?" Jennifer asked with a fond smile.

"Oh, I don't know," Theresa replied with a grin. "It seems to me I heard this crazy lady psychologist once tell it to a young man who used to live at Hamilton House."

"Did I really say something like that?"

"You really did."

"It just goes to show that I don't know everything."

"Oh, Jenny!" Theresa laughed and hugged her.

"So you really think I should go through with the weekend, huh?"

"I think you should go through with as many weekends and nights as you can."

"Boy, this chickens-and-frogs stuff can really wear you out," Jennifer said with a weary sigh.

"Only if you don't let them have their own way," Theresa said with a chuckle, and walked out of the room.

Trevor arrived home that evening and, with an abashed smile, handed Jennifer a huge bouquet.

"What are these for?" she asked in surprise.

"Penance."

"Penance?"

"For the note I sent with the painting. I was feeling...melancholy when I wrote it. Forgive me?"

Jennifer buried her face in the flowers, breathed in their beautiful mixture of scents and glanced up at him with sad eyes.

"This relationship will eventually have to end, Trevor."

"I know." He sighed and leaned against the wall. "I don't want it to, but I know it will. I realized that yesterday when we were at the construction site."

"It would probably be easier on both of us if we called everything to a halt right now," she stated reasonably.

He shrugged. "It probably would be, but I don't want to call a halt. I'll take what you can give me and be satisfied with it."

Her eyes searched his face, and she realized he meant what he said. He'd let her go when the time came, no matter how painful it was for both of them.

She laid the flowers on her desk, opened her arms and he was immediately in them, hugging her tightly and desperately, but she never noticed because she was hugging him back the same way.

The rest of the week continued in its normal routine. Jennifer began a heavy counseling schedule with Damien, which only confirmed what she'd already known. He was refusing to acknowledge that his mother was really gone. An added complication arose when Damien confessed that he wanted to go see where his mother was "sleeping" and that Trevor had refused to take him. In her heart, she knew that Damien had to visit his mother's grave, but she didn't know how to approach Trevor about the subject. She couldn't order him to take Damien to the cemetery, particularly when she wasn't certain Damien was emotionally strong enough to handle the reality.

They were, however, reaching a critical stage. The physical therapist had confided that even though Damien's exercises were giving him a longer lease, if he wasn't on his feet soon, there would be irreversible damage to his legs. Jennifer knew that she was going to have to take drastic measures, but with her emotions involved with both father and son, she was finding it difficult to take the needed steps toward a resolution.

On Thursday, she also realized there was a very large complication in her and Trevor's weekend plans. How would she explain to the kids that she was going away with Trevor? Her first inclination was to lie, but she knew Trevor was right when he'd said they knew what was going on. Somehow she had to convince them that it was all right for her not to practice what she preached.

She stewed about it all day and was a nervous wreck by the time evening came. Finally she called a general meeting and closed the doors to the community room. Everyone was present but Damien, who was in the kitchen with Theresa. Jennifer had decided that Damien should learn about his father's plans from Trevor.

She sat down cross-legged on the floor, stared at the kids sitting around her and made her explosive announcement. There was a long silence, which was finally broken by Sundance. The pretty girl, who was half Navaho, rested her elbows on her knees and her chin in her palms as she asked, "Are you in love with Trevor?"

"Yes," Jennifer admitted honestly. "But what I'm worried about is that all of you will think that you can do what I'm planning on doing, and it's important that you don't. I can sit here and say that you should do what I say and not what I do, but that isn't fair. I can also say that I'm an adult and you're not and that makes a difference, but again that isn't fair. Quite frankly, I don't know what to say to all of you, and that scares me."

Suddenly Long John burst into laughter and said, "How can we do what you're going to do? There's no way you'd ever let us go away for a weekend!"

"Yeah!" Another of the youngsters piped up.

Soon they were all laughing, and Racer caught Jennifer's hand and gave it a reassuring squeeze. "I think you worried yourself over nothing. We all know what's happening, and you were honest with us. That's all that matters."

"Oh, Racer, I hope you're right."

When Trevor sat down with Damien and explained that he and Jennifer were going away together for the weekend, Jennifer held her breath. She actually expected a replay of the tantrum that she'd witnessed that first day at Trevor's house. Therefore she was surprised when Damien wheeled himself into the kitchen, smiled at her and asked if she'd bring back a gift for Angel.

Touched, she knelt in front of him and hugged him tightly. He hugged her back and told her he loved her. She sat back on her heels, brushed the hair out of his eyes and told she loved him, too.

Finally Friday arrived. Trevor returned from the office in late afternoon, deposited their suitcases in the trunk of his car, and they left before the youngsters returned from school.

"Did you really think it was necessary to leave before the kids came home?" he asked after they'd driven nearly an hour in silence.

"Yes. They know what's happening, but I still think it's better this way. It's one thing to tell them what's going on, and it's quite another to give them a visual image."

"Jennifer, if you're really worried about this, I'll turn around and we'll go back to Hamilton House."

She glanced at his sober expression. "You really mean that, don't you?"

"Yes."

She smiled and tenderly laid her hand against his cheek. "Every time I think I know you, you surprise me again and show me how much I don't."

He smiled back, turned his head and pressed a kiss into her palm. "Are we going back or not? There's an exit up ahead."

"There's no way we're turning back, Trevor."

He released a relieved sigh and gruffly ordered, "Come here. You keep insisting on sitting a mile away from me."

They completed their drive, and Trevor let out a low whistle when they pulled up in front of the small A-frame cabin. "This is nice."

"I know. My dad used to bring me up here a lot, and I've never wanted to sell it. An elderly couple down the road take care of it for me. Come on in for the grand tour."

Trevor followed her in with the suitcases and a bag of groceries and set them on the floor. Jennifer took his hand and began the tour. Downstairs was the living room and kitchen combination and a bath, small guest room and tiny laundry room that sat behind the kitchen area.

It didn't take long to cover the first floor, and Jennifer hesitated at the bottom of the stairs that led up to the master bedroom. She glanced at Trevor shyly and asked, "Do you feel as nervous about this as I do right now?"

"Yes." He wrapped an arm around her and started her up the stairs. "Don't worry, Jenny. We don't have to do anything yet. You can show me the master bedroom in safety."

"Okay," she replied, sounding disappointed. He burst into laughter.

Upstairs she moved away from him, showed him the master bath and then turned back to gaze at the room.

"It's spartanly furnished but habitable, I guess," she said almost apologetically.

"All we really need is a bed," he teased as he wrapped his arms around her waist and pulled her against him. "Want to go for a walk?"

"A walk?"

"Uh-huh."

"A walk does sound kind of nice, doesn't it?"

"Sure. Plenty of fresh air, and we can catch the last of the sun if we hurry," he told her as he pulled her hair away from her neck and placed a kiss beneath it.

She shivered, and he kissed her again. With a moan she wrapped her arms around his neck and kissed him with all the pent-up longing that had been building inside her since the day they'd first met.

"Jennifer, we'll never make our walk if you keep this up," he rasped when she broke away from the kiss.

"Make love to me, Trevor."

"Oh, Jenny," he groaned. He caught her lips and swung her up into his arms.

He crossed to the bed and lowered her to it without ever breaking away from the kiss. She turned and molded herself to him when he came down beside her. The kiss seemed to go on forever, and when it finally ended they were both trembling. Trevor's hand moved to the front of her blouse, and he began to unbutton it, parting the fabric slowly and kissing each inch of flesh he revealed.

"You didn't wear a bra," he said when he pushed aside half the blouse and ran his hand from her breast to the feminine curve of her waist and back to her breast.

"I didn't want to waste time."

"Wanton," he teased as his hand cupped her breast and began to knead it sensuously.

She drew in a deep breath of pleasure and arched into his hand. He bent his head, placed a gentle kiss on the rose-tipped peak and then pushed the other side of her blouse away. She moaned deep in her throat as he cupped that breast with his other hand and began to knead it, also.

"Do you want me, Jenny?" he asked huskily.

"Yes."

"I'm glad," he whispered. He slid his hands beneath her shoulders, easing her up so he could remove her blouse.

"My turn," she whispered, and she reached for the buttons on his shirt. Her fingers were shaking so badly that she could barely work the buttons through the holes, but Trevor waited patiently, smiling down at her until she finally completed the task.

She ran her hands over the smooth, hard muscles of his chest and shivered. "You feel like steel satin, Trevor."

He growled and pulled her up against him, not even allowing her time to remove his shirt. She brushed her breasts against his bare chest, and he growled again, pushing her back down onto the mattress and raining tiny kisses around her breasts, moving torturously upward until she was nearly begging for him to take her into his mouth.

But he pulled away and drew in several gulps of air. "I have to slow down for a minute. Things are getting out of hand, Jenny." He touched her brow to ease the frown lines that appeared. "Let's take our time, sweetheart."

He dropped his hands to the snap of her jeans and opened it. Then he lowered the zipper, slipped his hands beneath the denim and slid her jeans down over her hips. She kicked off her shoes as he eased the fabric down her legs, his eyes feasting on her thighs and calves. He finally pulled the pants off and dropped them to the floor before removing her socks and gently kneading her feet. "You have beautiful feet, Jenny. They're as beautifully shaped as the rest of you."

He lowered his head, kissed the arch of each foot and then sat back on the bed and let his gaze roam up her. His visual caress was as volatile as any touch, and she shivered and raised her arms, beckoning him to come to her.

"In a minute," he said, and he slipped his hands beneath the elastic of the lace panties that still covered her hips.

A tremor shook him as he once again let his gaze roam over her, and he reverently said, "You're Aphrodite on a bed, Jennifer Anne Hamilton."

"Come to me, Trevor," she whispered.

He nodded but stood, dropped his shirt and lowered his hands to the front of his jeans. Her pulse began to pound and her tongue slipped out to wet parched lips as her gaze anchored itself on the waistband of his jeans. A fine, almost invisible trail of hair began just below his navel and disappeared seductively beneath the denim.

Her breathing became shallow as she watched him release his belt buckle and the snap on his jeans. Her eyes followed the path of his fingers as he lowered the zipper on his pants, and she drew in a deep breath and held it as he kicked off his shoes and let his pants drop to the floor. His socks quickly followed, but when he caught his thumb in the waistband of his shorts, she came up on her knees.

"Let me, Trevor."

He stepped forward, and his eyes were pools of deep purple.

She trailed her hands over his shoulders and down his chest before slipping her fingers beneath the elastic. She paused to lean forward and tongue a hard, male nipple and then lowered his briefs over his hips.

Instead of coming to her, as she expected, he stood before her, looking a little uncertain.

"Come here," she ordered, smiling up at him.

He stared down into her eyes. Then his gaze lowered. She'd tossed back the covers and sat framed in pristine white. His eyes feasted on her breasts, the feminine curve of her waist and the soft swell of her stomach before dropping to her shapely thighs and the brilliant copper curls that beckoned from between them.

He closed his eyes tightly and swallowed hard. He was in such a raging fever of desire that it almost frightened him. Never had the physical act of love been so important, nor had he ever wanted it to be so very special for a woman.

"What is it, Trevor?" Jennifer asked.

His eyes snapped open, and he cleared his throat before he could find his voice.

"I don't know how much control I'm going to be able to exercise. I've never wanted anyone the way I want you right now."

She caught his hand, giving it a gentle tug.

"Come to bed, Trevor."

He groaned and lay down beside her. They both released sighs of exquisite pleasure as warm, naked flesh met with warm, naked flesh from shoulder to knee. Her hands began to explore him, and he rolled to his back, bringing her over him. His hands tangled in the rich depths of her copper hair, and he brought her face down to him so he could rain thousands of tiny kisses from her forehead to the delicate curve of her chin.

She let out a small sigh, and her head dropped back when his lips moved on to the velvet regions of her throat and neck. Suddenly he groaned and rolled again, pulling her beneath him, and his lips captured a rosy nipple and drew it into his mouth, his tongue flicking over it with quick, tantalizing strokes.

"Trevor!" she gasped, and arched feverishly toward him.

"Easy," he soothed, and he trailed kisses from her breast to her throat, where he pressed an ardent kiss to her rapidly beating pulse and then trailed kisses down to her other breast.

"Oh!" she cried out when he began to treat that breast to the same delights. His hands seemed to be everywhere at once, honing in on every erogenous zone, and she began to move frantically beneath him.

"Trevor, I can't stand it," she panted when his lips began trailing down her abdomen. "I need you now!"

A shudder raced through him at the hoarse plea in her voice, and he rested a flushed cheek against her stomach.

"Jenny, we have to slow down. If I come to you right now, it's going to be over before it has a chance to begin."

"Love me, Trevor," she begged softly, catching his shoulders with her hands and trying to urge him upward. "Please love me."

"Jenny, I'm on fire for you. I won't be able to hold back. I—"

"I'm on fire, too," she interrupted, again trying to urge him upward.

He raised himself up to his elbows, and his eyes traveled from her abdomen to the aroused peaks of her heaving breasts. His throat went dry as his gaze moved to her face. The passion in her eyes made his heart hesitate and then leap into a frantic, thumping beat.

He forced himself to move upward, his strength returning as her silken thighs parted in invitation and her hips rose toward him eagerly. With a groan he joined them, his lips closing over hers to capture the passionate gasp that escaped her trembling lips.

They lay there, linked, for what seemed an eternity, and then Trevor whispered, "I love you, Jenny." And he began to move inside her.

Her arms wrapped around his neck, and she brought his lips into contact with hers, kissing him with every ounce of love that existed within her as he led her through an indescribable journey that only a man and woman in love can share.

Chapter Nine

They spent the remainder of Friday night and all day Saturday, laughing, playing and loving. Trevor couldn't remember ever feeling so uninhibited, and each time he looked at Jennifer, he fell more deeply in love. It was a poignant love because he knew it would have to end, and yet he kept telling himself that there had to be a way for them to be together. Maybe if he kept telling himself that, he'd find a way.

When Jennifer suggested a walk late Saturday afternoon, he agreed, and hand in hand they began to explore the surrounding countryside. They climbed a small hill as the sun began to set and found themselves in an old, ill-kempt cemetery.

Jennifer entered the area and moved through it, stopping to trail her fingers over crumbling headstones as she tried to make out names and dates that had been worn by the elements until they were almost invisible.

"It looks sad. So forgotten," she murmured as she stood gazing down at one toppled headstone.

"Most of the dates here are before the turn of the century. Many of these people have probably been forgotten."

Jennifer nodded and leaned her head against his shoulder as he draped his arm around her. Suddenly she found the strength to approach the subject that had been nagging at her.

"Trevor, why haven't you taken Damien to visit his mother's grave?"

He stiffened against her. "It would upset him too much."

"But he wants to go, Trevor."

"It would upset him too much," he repeated.

"It would be traumatic," she agreed, "But he needs to understand what has happened to her, Trevor. You told him that his mother went to sleep so she could be with the angels. That's a very good explanation to help a child understand death, but often when a child attends the funeral, he's better able to realize that it's a permanent kind of sleep. Damien wasn't able to attend his mother's funeral, and he still believes she can wake up. A visit to the cemetery could help him understand that she can't."

"You're not really suggesting that I take him to the cemetery, are you?"

"Yes," she answered. "Remember when I said yesterday that telling the kids what was going on and giving them a visual image were two different things?"

"Yes."

"Well, in this instance, I think Damien needs a visual image."

Trevor released a long breath and shook his head. "I don't know if I can do what you're suggesting, Jennifer."

"I'll be there to help you, Trevor. Damien needs this. I'm certain of it."

He leaned his head against hers and nodded. "All right, Jenny. If you'll be there to help me, I'll do it."

They stood there with their arms linked around each other, gazing over the ancient cemetery that, despite its crumbling and lonely appearance, emanated a quiet peace. When the sun finally set, they turned and made their way back to the cabin.

The first thing Jennifer was aware of as she stirred toward wakefulness early Sunday morning was a sweltering heat. The second thing was a prickling sensation along the length of her body. Lazily she opened her eyes, and a contented smile curved her lips.

"What are you doing?" she questioned sleepily.

Trevor sat next to her on the bed, cross-legged, his elbows on his knees and his chin cradled in his hands. A fire burned cheerfully in the freestanding fireplace located in a corner behind him, casting a rosy glow over his naked, sun-bronzed body. His eyes were warm pools of violet as he gazed at her, and his lips were curved in a satisfied grin.

"I'm memorizing every nook and cranny of you," he answered. "Are you cold without the covers?"

"No. In fact, it's hot in here. You build a nice fire."

His smile turned boyish. "Fire making was the only merit badge I earned in Boy Scouts."

"You were a Boy Scout?"

He laughed. "Not for long. They kicked me out for being unruly."

"I think you're the first man I've ever met who flunked Boy Scouts." She chuckled.

"I hope I'm a first at many things as far as you're concerned." He began to stroke her thigh. "I thought you'd never wake up."

She covered her mouth and yawned. "Have you been awake long?"

"Hours."

"Hmm. I bet you're hungry."

He caught her hand and brought it to his lips, pressing a kiss to her knuckles. "Ravenous."

"You could have raided the refrigerator."

"I did. It didn't have what I wanted."

"And just what was it you wanted?"

"Three guesses, and the first five don't count," he answered as he stretched out beside her and pulled her purposefully into his arms. "You, Jennifer Anne, are a piece of art. If ever a man needed proof that there really is a God, all he'd have to do is look at you. Only a supreme being could make something this perfect."

"The many faces of Dr. Trevor Hawke," she murmured as she cradled his face between her hands and gazed at him lovingly. "The healer, the artist and the poet."

"You left out the lover," he admonished huskily as his hand swept down her length.

Her eyes danced with teasing deviltry. "As an old lawyer friend of mine would say, the jury's still out on that one. You've argued your case brilliantly, but I think I need a final summation before I can make up my mind."

"Oh?" he growled as he rolled her to her back and glared at her in mock indignation. "Well, we'll just have to get a final verdict on that, won't we, Dr. Hamilton?"

She opened her mouth to speak, only to have him take advantage of her parted lips by capturing them and gliding his tongue inside. His kiss was explosive, and his hands roamed over her in a sensual exploration designed to drive her to madness. When she was certain she couldn't bear another moment, Trevor rose above her and whispered raggedly, "Let's just see what that jury has to say."

He joined them with a carefully leashed passion, and suddenly they were being plunged back through time and then spiraling toward the future. The sun rose and set. The moon rose and set. And through it all, the fire burned, raging out of control.

A moan escaped Jennifer's lips, and her arms locked around his neck, dragging him down for her fevered kiss. Their travels continued until they were finally leaping into heaven and then beyond into eternity.

"And the lover," she whispered against his lips as they came tumbling back to the present. "Oh, definitely the lover."

When it was finally time to leave, both Jennifer and Trevor eyed the cabin sadly.

"I wish we could stay longer," she said as they stood beside the car.

"Me, too, but we can come back." He kissed her temple.

"This has been such a special time for me, Trevor." She gazed up at him tenderly. "I'll never come here again that I won't remember you."

"Hey! Don't write me off yet. Our days are hardly numbered."

He was wrong, and they both knew it, but she didn't remind him. Instead she smiled, stroked his cheek and said, "I love you, Trevor Hawke. Thank you for a wonderful weekend."

"I love you, Jennifer Hamilton, and you're welcome," he replied. He gave her a big hug before finally saying, "It's time to go."

"I know."

Reluctantly he opened the door and let her slide in ahead of him. Even more reluctantly, he started the engine and turned the car back toward Los Angeles. He had a feeling that the good times had just ended and the bad times were looming right in front of him.

It was only the memory of that peaceful weekend that helped Jennifer survive during the next ten days. Four new runaways arrived at Hamilton House between Monday morning and Tuesday night. Two of them would be going home by the end of the week. One had easily fit into the schedule of Hamilton House, but the last one, the difficult child from the other halfway house, was trying Jennifer's patience to the limits. To top it off, Damien had once again decided to become recalcitrant and seemed to purposely disobey her every order.

It was after midnight when she finally collapsed at the kitchen table and rested her head in her hands. She was too tired even to try to climb the stairs. When she heard Trevor enter through the front door, she forced herself to her feet and crossed to the kitchen door. He looked as weary as she felt, and she smiled at him solicitously.

"Bad day?"

"Awful," he muttered. He gave her a hug. "I didn't get out of surgery until two hours ago."

"Oh, Trevor," she commiserated, brushing his hair out of his eyes.

He sighed and leaned his beard-stubbled cheek against her forehead. "You feel good. Smell good, too."

"You smell like antiseptic."

He chuckled and dropped a quick kiss to her lips. "I've missed you so much. Every night I lie in bed and wish you were in my arms."

"I know."

"So when are my wishes going to come true?"

She glanced up at him and smiled. "How about now?"

"Now?"

"If we were really quiet, tiptoed upstairs to my room and you promised to be gone before dawn..."

"Dawn isn't too far away, but I'm game if you are."

"I'm game, but you look so exhausted, Trevor."

"So do you." He smiled wryly. "Before we managed to do anything, we'd probably both fall asleep and get caught red-handed."

"Probably." She chuckled.

"Maybe I could take a rain check and tiptoe upstairs tomorrow night," he suggested, arching a brow rakishly.

She sighed and leaned against him contentedly. "I think that could be arranged."

"Mmm." He kissed her tenderly, passionately. "Tomorrow night, then."

"Tomorrow night," she repeated as he began to urge her up the stairs.

The next morning Damien and Jennifer once again butted heads. First he wouldn't eat his breakfast. Then he wouldn't dress for school. She finally confronted him in her office, crossed her arms over her chest and tapped her foot impatiently.

"Damien, for the past week you have been behaving like a bear with a bee sting on the end of his nose. Why?"

His lower lip thrust out, and he glanced away from her in belligerent silence.

"Damien, I asked you a question, and I would appreciate it if you would answer me."

"I don't like you anymore."

"Okay, I'll buy that. Why don't you like me anymore?"

She was prepared for a confrontation over the time she'd spent with his father and was surprised when he said, "Because you never talk to me."

"Never talk to you?" she repeated. "Damien, I talk to you every day."

"Not like you used to. You're always with those other people, and I don't like them."

Her lips began to twitch when she realized he was jealous of the new runaways she'd been devoting so much time to. "Well, no one says you have to like them, Damien, but it's too bad you don't. They're very nice people and would like to be friends with you. You can never have too many friends, you know."

"I still don't like them," he muttered.

"Well, that's fine with me. Why don't you get dressed for school?"

He opened his mouth as if to object, but then closed it and nodded. Jennifer walked out of the room.

"Figure out what his problem is?" Theresa asked when Jennifer wandered into the kitchen.

"Good old-fashioned jealousy. He doesn't think he's getting the attention from me that he should be getting."

Theresa nodded and said, "He's becoming very attached to you, Jenny. Maybe too attached."

"Too attached?"

"He's already lost one mother, Jenny. What's going to happen when he loses her substitute?"

Jennifer collapsed into a kitchen chair and stared at Theresa in consternation. "You think he's getting that close to me?"

"You love him, Jenny, and you love his father. What do *you* think?"

"That I'd better be getting him onto his feet very soon," she replied quietly, shaken by Theresa's revelation and wondering why she hadn't realized it herself. It was one thing to indulge herself in an affair with Trevor. It was quite another to let Damien become dependent upon her when she knew she'd never become a permanent part of his life. As Theresa had so succinctly stated, he'd already lost one mother. Losing a substitute mother could be devastating.

She'd planned to discuss Damien with Trevor right after supper, but he called and informed her he was going to be late.

"Is my rain check still good?" he asked huskily.

"Depends on how late you're going to be."

"Will you wait for me in your bed?"

"You're going to be that late?"

"I won't be burning the midnight oil, but I probably won't be home until after head count."

"Then I suppose that's where I'll be waiting, but I need to talk to you, Trevor."

"Is something wrong?" he immediately asked in concern.

"Not exactly," she hedged, "but I do need to talk to you."

"We'll talk. See you later."

"I'll be waiting."

Trevor was late, and Jennifer nervously awaited his arrival, jumping at every creak the old building made, certain that the entire population of Hamilton House was wide-awake and would hear him creeping into her room.

When she heard the front door open and close, she sat up in bed and listened. It seemed every footfall was a cannon shot and it took him forever to reach her room. She was ready to crawl under the bed and hide by the time the door eased open.

Trevor gazed into the room, and a smile curved his lips.

"What took you so long?" she whispered.

"I made a bed check of my own," he whispered back as he approached the side of the bed and gazed lovingly down at her. "Everyone is sound asleep with visions of sugar plums dancing in their heads. You can stop biting your nails, Jenny."

She immediately jerked her thumbnail away from her lips and gave him a wry smile. "You really do know me too well, Trevor."

"When I make love to you, sweetheart, I want your entire attention," he stated as he slipped out of his jacket and dropped it onto the chair beside her bed.

He sat down on the edge and lowered the sheet she'd tucked around herself. His eyes flared brightly and then rose to her face.

"This is a sexy nightgown, Jennifer. Did you wear it just for me?"

"Yes," she whispered, glancing down shyly.

"It's a beautiful wrapping, but I like the package inside better," he said as he caught her chin, raised her head and pressed a kiss to her lips. "Why are you suddenly so shy?"

She shrugged. "I don't know. Nervous, I guess."

"Everyone's asleep, Jennifer. I really did check."

"I know. Thank you."

"We'll be quiet. I promise."

She arched a doubtful brow, and he chuckled.

"Come here," he ordered, and tugged her into his arms. The minute they wrapped around her and his lips came down over hers, all her shyness and worry fled. Hungrily she kissed him back, until with a groan he released her and began to tug at his clothes.

He wasn't getting them off fast enough for her, and she began to help. Finally he was standing beside her bed, naked and blatantly aroused.

"I've missed you so," he whispered as he crawled in beside her and stripped the nightgown over her head. "I've missed you so much."

Before she could respond, his lips came down over hers, and he led her back into the world of passion that they had discovered together.

When they finally lay side by side, spent and replete, Trevor kissed her forehead and murmured, "What was it you wanted to talk to me about, Jenny?"

She shook her head to clear away the drowsiness assaulting her. "Damien. He's getting too close to me, Trevor."

He frowned and blessed the darkness that hid it. "Is there something wrong with that?"

"Yes. Theresa thinks he's substituting me for his mother, and I can't allow that to happen. He's had enough trauma by losing his mother, Trevor. Losing me would only compound that trauma. We have to get him back on his feet, and the sooner the better. The only way to do that is to prove to him that his mother is never coming home, whether he stays in a wheelchair or not."

Trevor swallowed the lump that had formed in his throat. When Damien left Hamilton House, that meant he left, too, and he wondered how he could live through every day without seeing Jennifer. "I see. So what do you suggest?"

"I want to take him to visit his mother's grave as soon as possible. What is your schedule like?"

Full forever, he wanted to scream. But he knew he couldn't. He could never trade his son's health for his happiness. "Barring any emergencies, I should be through at the office by two tomorrow afternoon."

That soon! Jennifer wanted to wail. Instead she closed her eyes and said, "That's good. Let's plan on tomorrow. We can go right after Damien gets home from school."

"Are you sure this will help, Jennifer?"

"No," she whispered, "but I'm praying that it will."

"Could it make him worse?"

"Yes," she admitted, "but I think Damien is emotionally strong enough to handle it. He's been in counseling since the accident, and he's grown a lot since he's come here.''

"What do you expect to happen?" he asked dully.

"I expect tears, anger, depression, more tantrums. I expect him to regress for a time, but I think that once he's resigned himself to the fact that his mother is gone and will never come back, he'll be ready to let me help him bury his guilt so that he can walk again.''

"What will I need to do tomorrow?"

"I want you to call me just before you leave the office. That will give me time to get him dressed and prepare him for where we're going. Did his mother have a favorite flower?''

"Pink roses."

"I'll buy some pink roses, then. We'll drive him to the cemetery and let him put them on her grave. From that point on I'll have to play it by ear.''

"Would it be a good idea to bring Angel with us?"

"I don't know," Jennifer replied. "I'll have to think about that.''

"I'm afraid, Jenny."

"You don't have to be afraid. I'll be right there with you.''

He didn't confess that his real fear was that once Damien accepted his mother's loss, Trevor would be losing Jennifer. He groaned and rolled against her, his body declaring its unquenchable thirst for her, and once again they explored the world of passion that existed between them.

The next afternoon Trevor sat tensely eyeing the clock in his office and finally gulped, picked up the phone and made his call to Jennifer.

Jennifer hung up and walked toward the community room in search of Damien. He and Angel were bent over a game of checkers, and Jennifer frowned, wondering if Trevor's suggestion that they bring the girl along was a good one.

"Angel, could I speak with you a moment?"

"Sure," Angel answered.

"I'd like to speak with you alone," Jennifer stated.

Angel looked confused but nodded and followed Jennifer to her office. Jennifer sat down behind her desk and told the girl what she and Trevor planned to do.

The girl's dark eyes filled with tears, and she asked, "Does he have to go, Jenny?"

"Yes, Angel, he does," Jennifer answered. Then she drew in a deep breath. "Would you like to go with us?"

Angel gnawed on her bottom lip and finally said, "Yes."

"All right. I'm going to talk to Damien and tell him what's about to happen. I'll tell him that you're going with us."

Angel nodded. "I should wear a dress. I'll go upstairs and change."

"You're a wonder," Jennifer murmured under her breath as she watched the girl walk out of the room.

Jennifer returned to the community room, sat down in Angel's chair at the checkerboard and said, "Damien, you need to change your clothes and put on your suit."

"Why?" he asked in surprise.

"Because your dad is on his way here, and you and he and Angel and I are all going to go to the cemetery to put some flowers on your mother's grave."

The emotions flew across his face so fast that Jennifer couldn't decipher them. "I'm going to go see Mama?" he finally whispered.

"Yes, Damien," she said quietly.

"I don't want to go."

Jennifer sat back in her chair and frowned. "I thought you wanted to go see your mother, Damien."

"I do, but..."

"But what, Damien?" she encouraged.

"What if she doesn't want to come home with me, Jenny?"

Jennifer gulped as she frantically searched for a response to his question. Finally she decided that honesty was all she could offer him.

"Damien, your mother is not going to come home with you."

"But I want her to come home," he said as tears began to roll down his cheeks. "I want her to be with me. I love her, Jenny."

Jennifer reached across the table and wiped the tears from his cheeks. "I know you do, Damien, and she will always be here with you in spirit."

"Do I have to go?"

"You don't have to go visit her today, but someday you should go." She gave him an encouraging smile and said, "I'm going to leave this decision up to you. If you want to go see your mother, then we'll go today. If you don't, then we'll go another day."

He looked so forlorn that Jennifer crossed to his side and knelt beside him. He flung his arms around her neck and sobbed as if his heart were broken. Finally he sniffed, pulled away from her and, with a hint of the man he would someday become, said, "I'd better put on my suit."

"Would you like me to help you?"

He nodded, and Jennifer stepped behind his chair and wheeled him to her office.

When Trevor stepped through the front door of Hamilton House, he was greeted by a quiet, solemn group. Both Angel and Jennifer wore dresses. Damien had on his blue suit and had a florist's box resting across his legs. He glanced up at his father, his eyes red and swollen and his cheeks tear stained.

Trevor felt as if someone had just punched a hole in his chest and ripped out his heart. He automatically took a step toward his son and then hesitated, glancing toward Jennifer.

She gave an almost imperceptible shake of her head and stated, "Damien's ready to go."

Trevor had to swallow hard several times to remove the lump in his throat so he could speak, and still his voice was hoarse when he responded with "Fine."

Angel wheeled Damien's chair out to the car, where Trevor settled him into the front seat. Jennifer placed the flowers on Damien's lap before she joined Angel in the back.

The group drove in complete silence to the cemetery, which was lush and green and carefully tended. A far cry from the one she and Trevor had visited. When they drove past a funeral in progress, Damien quickly averted his head and closed his eyes, not opening them again until Trevor finally pulled the car to a stop.

Silently Trevor got out of the car, retrieved Damien's wheelchair from the trunk and brought it to the door. He opened the door, lifted Damien out and settled him into the chair. He wheeled Damien this time, and Jennifer and Angel followed. When they reached

Patricia Hawke's grave, Trevor brought Damien's chair to a stop and knelt down beside him.

"That's not my mother," Damien whispered tearfully. He shook his head, as if by shaking it the denial would be the truth.

"Yes, Damien, it is," Trevor stated softly. He brushed some dried leaves and twigs off the grass-covered grave and then reached up to run his fingers across the headstone. "You can read, Damien. Read it to me."

"No!" Damien exclaimed harshly. "I want to go home. Take me home! That's not my mother!"

"Damien, read what it says on the headstone," Trevor ordered quietly.

"I don't want to!" he exclaimed, tears rolling down his cheeks. "Jenny, I don't want to!"

Angel was now crying silently and wrapped her arm around Jennifer's waist. Jennifer held the girl to her side and said, "You don't have to read it, Damien, but it's not going to change the truth."

She released Angel and settled on her knees beside him. "Damien, have you ever been to the mountains in the fall when the leaves turn yellow and red?"

He sniffed and nodded.

"Do you know why they change color?"

He sniffed again and shook his head.

"In the fall the leaves die, and they change from green to yellow and red. They fall to the ground, and in the spring the tree grows new leaves. Some people call that a renewal of life. It means that life begins all over again."

He was staring at her intently, and she caught his hand and held it. "People are sort of like those leaves, Damien. The difference is that people have spirits, and no one knows where those spirits go, but most of us believe they go somewhere very beautiful and very special.''

"They go to join the angels?'' he asked.

"I don't know for certain, Damien. All I know is that your mother loved you very, very much, and nothing or no one will ever take her love away from you.''

"She went away because of me,'' he whispered as new tears began to flow down his cheeks. "I made her go away.''

"No, Damien,'' Jennifer stated firmly. "Your mother was in an accident. What happened to her was not your fault.''

"She's not ever coming home, is she?'' he asked forlornly as he stared at the grave.

"No, Damien, she's not going to come home,'' Jennifer answered.

He shook his head so hard that his tears were flung into the air. "It's not true!'' he cried. "It's not true!''

"Yes, Damien, it is true,'' Trevor told him and laid his hand on his arm. "It is true.''

"But I don't want it to be true! I want my mama to come home.''

"Damien, I don't want it to be true, either, but it is.'' Trevor caught Damien's head between his hands, forcing him to look at him. "Damien, I love you, and if there were any way I could bring your mother home to you, I would. But there isn't.''

Damien stared at the grave and shook his head. Trevor took the flower box from Damien's lap and laid it on the ground. Then he lifted his son out of his chair and settled him on the ground beside him. Carefully Trevor opened the box and placed a single pink rose on the grave. He lifted the second rose and placed it into Damien's hand.

"Give her the rose, Damien," he told him.

Damien's hand trembled so violently that Trevor grasped it to still it. Then he gently urged Damien's hand forward. When Damien's hand rested just above the rose Trevor had placed on the grave, Trevor released his hold and Damien laid his own rose beside his father's.

"I love you, Mama," he whispered as the tears poured down his cheeks. "Be happy with the angels."

Jennifer rose to her feet, and Angel moved to her side and buried her face against Jennifer's chest as she sobbed. Jennifer's arms wrapped around her and held her. Trevor's arms wrapped around his son, and he rocked him and murmured to him as they cried together in grief.

Jennifer closed her eyes and uttered a silent prayer for both her own father and Damien's mother and then one for all the people present. When she was through, she led Angel back to the car, where they sat for more than an hour before Trevor and Damien returned.

Again the car was silent as the group drove back to Hamilton House. Damien had buried his mother. Now Jennifer prayed that she'd be able to make him walk again.

Chapter Ten

When the group returned to Hamilton House, Damien rolled himself into Jennifer's office and sat gazing out the window. He was still there late that night after everyone had gone to bed.

Trevor stood in the doorway, and Jennifer moved to his side and wrapped an arm around his waist. He automatically draped an arm around her shoulders and gave a forlorn shake of his head.

"He won't talk to me, Jenny. He just sits there and stares out the window. I don't think he even hears what I'm saying when I try to talk to him."

She gave his waist a reassuring squeeze and eased him away from the doorway. When she'd led him to a spot where she knew Damien couldn't hear them, she said, "He hears what you're saying Trevor. He's just grieving right now, and he needs to grieve. He'll be like this for a few days, and then he's going to become unruly and angry. If you thought his temper tantrums were bad before, they're going to be a hundred times worse now. After he goes through that stage, he's going to cry. Once he starts crying, we'll know we've won the battle.''

He rested his head against hers and sighed. ''I hate putting him through this. I hated taking him there today.''

''I know,'' she consoled, ''but we had to do it. It was the only way to make him really face up to the fact that his mother is gone.''

''I don't want him to be alone tonight.''

''He's not going to be alone. You're going to carry him up to my room, and both of us are going to stay with him.''

Trevor raised his head and gazed down at her, his wry smile reflecting a hint of his usual good nature. ''Grown-up people who are not married do not sleep in the same bed, Jennifer.''

''Tommy's mom and her boyfriend do,'' she responded with a teasing smile. ''Damien's so upset that he's never going to know the difference. All he'll know is that two people who love him very much are with him. Get him ready for bed and carry him upstairs, okay?''

''I'd never turn down an opportunity to share your bed, Jennifer, even if my son is sleeping between us. What about the other kids?''

''We'll leave the door open. If they have any doubts, they'll be able to peek inside.''

Trevor nodded and went into the office to prepare his son for bed. Jennifer spent some time with Angel, assuring the teary-eyed girl that Damien was going to be all right. By the time she arrived at her room, Trevor was already in bed with Damien, and he gave her a halfhearted lecherous grin. Damien just lay there, staring up at the ceiling.

Jennifer pulled a long, sedate cotton nightgown from her drawer and took it into the bath, where she changed. She returned to her room and climbed into bed, putting her arm around Damien's waist. With a muffled sob he rolled against her, buried his head against her chest and clung to her tightly.

Trevor glanced at her with a morose expression, and Jennifer knew it hurt him that his son wouldn't turn to him for comfort. She tried to give him a reassuring smile, but it didn't erase the pain in his eyes. He slid down into the bed, turned out the bedside light and lay staring at the ceiling as Damien had done earlier.

Jennifer closed her eyes and fought back the tears that threatened. She'd lost her heart to both the male Hawkes, and when they hurt, she hurt with them. She soothingly stroked Damien's hair and wished she could do the same for Trevor. But he lay quietly on his side of the bed, as far removed from her emotionally as he was by distance.

When Damien's breathing had deepened and his hold around her relaxed, Jennifer whispered, "Trevor, are you awake?"

"Yes."

"You should get some sleep. You have a long day ahead of you tomorrow."

"I don't have surgery tomorrow. I'll be all right."

They were quiet for a long time before he whispered, "Jenny?"

"Yes."

"Nothing."

"What did you want to say, Trevor?"

"I...I was just wishing that you didn't have to move so far away. I was wishing you could choose a site for your new Hamilton House closer to me so we could be together."

Her eyes blinked closed, and she let out a weary sigh. "And how close would it have to be, Trevor? You know as well as I do that even a closer site in the country with the amount of land I need would be more than an hour's drive away. Would you want to commute that distance each way every time you had to go to the hospital for an emergency?"

He turned to his side and gazed at her in question. "Do you have to move to the country? Why can't you stay in the city?"

"Because the country is a healthier atmosphere. These kids need to get out of the city and away from the pressures here. They need fresh air, sunshine and lots of room to roam."

Again a long silence passed before he propped himself up on one elbow and stared at her. His expression was shielded by the darkness, but she could still see the almost desperate gleam in his violet eyes.

"I love you, Jenny. Damien loves you. What are we going to do when we lose you?"

She shook her head against the pillow and reached up to touch his cheek. "Trevor, don't do this to us. We knew in the beginning that it would have to end. I've already started construction. I've already spent a fortune, and—"

"Jennifer, I don't care about the money," he interrupted. "I'll reimburse you for the money. Just don't leave us. Please don't leave us. We need you just as much or more than these kids do. I know I swore I'd never ask this, but give up your new Hamilton House and marry me. Be my wife and Damien's mother.''

Tears filled her eyes and began to spill down her cheeks. He reached out and tenderly brushed them away, but they still continued to fall.

"I love you, Trevor. I love Damien. But I can't walk away from Hamilton House. These kids are what I am and what I'll always be. Without them I'd dry up and blow away in the wind.''

She once again touched his cheek and gave him a wavering smile. "If I gave up my career for you and Damien, I'd eventually end up hating you for it. Just as you'd end up hating me if you gave up yours. We're dedicated professionals with talents that can't be wasted. Despite our personal feelings, we have callings that are too strong for us to ignore. We are what we are, and our love can't change that.''

"There has to be a way, Jenny. There has to be a compromise in here that will allow us to have our careers and each other, too.''

"If you can find a compromise, I'll listen to it, Trevor, but I think you're wasting your time. I've always dreamed of moving Hamilton House to the country, and I'm moving it to the country. As much as that land means to me, I'd give it up for you if I thought giving it up would be the solution. Even with our combined fortunes, we'd never be able to find the amount of land I need far enough removed from the city to satisfy me and close enough to allow you a decent response time to the hospital, and we both know it.''

"I could live in the city during the week and on those weekends I'm on call. Then I'd spend my free weekends with you. Some marriages thrive on times apart, Jenny. Maybe ours would.''

"No," Jennifer denied sadly. "I'm not made like that, Trevor. If I'm married, then I want a husband. I want him there at night to listen to the successes or failures I've had during the day, and I want to be able to listen to his successes or failures. Every time you came home for a weekend, I'd feel guilty, as if I weren't giving you the support that I should. I'd also hate the goodbyes every Sunday night. I've never been good at handling goodbyes, Trevor.''

"So what's the answer, Jenny?"

"The same one that's been there all along, Trevor. When I move to the country, we end.''

He fell back down on his pillow and flung his arm over his eyes. "I hate that answer, Jenny.''

"Do you have a different one?"

"No.''

"I wish it could be different.''

"So do I, but I won't bring the subject up again unless I can offer you a viable compromise. I promise. Just give me everything you can until that day finally arrives.''

"That's a promise I can make, Trevor.''

Five days passed, and Damien was still quiet and withdrawn. Jennifer began to fret, now wondering if he'd been as strong emotionally as she'd thought. Maybe she'd made the wrong decision, pushed him too hard. Maybe she'd damaged him irrevocably. On the fifth night she was almost physically ill with worry. Damien had returned to his cot in the office, and when the soft knock on her bedroom sounded, she sat up, almost praying that the boy had gone berserk and destroyed the entire downstairs.

She called for entrance and then smiled despite her worry when the door opened and Trevor stood there in pajama bottoms, an almost shy expression on his face.

"Hi," he said softly.

"Hi, yourself."

"May I come in?"

"Sure."

"I need a hug," he informed her as he stepped into the room and closed the door behind him.

"Oh, Trevor," she replied, and opened her arms.

He was instantly in them, and he buried his face against her neck. "Is he ever going to talk to me, Jenny?"

"Of course he is," she assured him.

"I need you, Jenny. I need to make love to you."

"Then come to bed," she said, tossing back the sheet and giving him an inviting smile.

"How I love you," he whispered as his eyes moved over her in a passionate exploration.

"I love you, too," she whispered back. "Take off my clothes and make wild, abandoned love to me, Trevor."

"Lady, you've got a deal," he replied, and he quickly stripped the top of her shorty pajamas over her head.

The next morning when her alarm went off, Jennifer groaned, pulled her pillow over her head, then finally acknowledged it and turned it off. She sighed half in weariness and half in repleteness. Trevor had made love to her not once, but twice before he'd finally slipped from her bed.

There was a new touch to their lovemaking now, as if they were both determined to build up a lifetime of memories.

She stretched, flinching slightly at her sore muscles, and then climbed from the bed. She showered, dressed and went downstairs. All the kids had left for school except Damien and Angel. Despite his withdrawal, Damien still dressed every morning and went to school without complaint. Since Angel always walked with him, she was always one of the last to leave.

Jennifer strolled into the kitchen, gave everyone a cheerful good morning and poured herself a cup of coffee. She almost let out a whoop of joy when Damien suddenly exploded into a rage behind her. It had been a small matter that had finally set him off. Theresa had put raspberry instead of strawberry jam on his toast.

The toast landed on the floor, and the jar of raspberry jam crashed against the wall. Jennifer stood leaning against the counter smiling as Damien screamed and threw everything within his reach. Both Theresa and Angel stared at her as if she'd just gone crazy when she didn't step in to control the tantrum.

When Damien was finally done, Jennifer picked up a broom and dustpan and started sweeping up the broken pieces of glass. When that was accomplished, she wet a rag, extended it toward Damien and ordered him to clean the jam off the wall.

"I will not," he stated stubbornly, and folded his arms over his chest.

"You will, too," Jennifer stated just as stubbornly and forced the rag into his hands.

"I hate you," he told her.

"I don't care. You still have to clean up the wall."

"My dad hates you."

"I don't care. You still have to clean up the wall."

"I won't go to school."

"I don't care. You still have to clean up the wall."

He glared at her, and Jennifer leaned next to the jam smear and waited patiently.

Finally it was Angel who defused the battle of wills. "Damien, I have to leave for school in just a few minutes," she informed the boy. "If you haven't cleaned the wall, then I'll have to leave without you."

He glanced uncertainly at Angel, and she shrugged eloquently. He glared once again at Jennifer but washed off the wall and was ready to leave in a matter of minutes.

When he returned from school, there were two more explosive tantrums, and Trevor walked in on the middle of the last one. He stood inside the doorway, his mouth gaping as he watched his son hurl a small potted Swedish ivy through the closed window of the community room. A second later he was in the middle of the fracas, and it was several minutes before the situation was under control.

Trevor met Jennifer in the hallway, grabbed her and gave her a bear hug. "Jenny, I know this sounds awful, but do you know how wonderful it was to hear him say he hated me?"

She laughed, hugged him back and nodded. "We just hit stage two, Trevor. Stage three is just around the corner."

"And then?" he questioned quietly, leaning her back so he could stare down into her face.

"And then we get him onto his feet. Before you know it, your son is going to be walking again."

Trevor's heart was torn between joy and pain as he gazed down into her upturned, smiling face. He wanted his son to walk more than anything in the world, but he knew that when he did, it would be the beginning of the end for him and Jennifer.

He hugged her tightly, kissed her passionately and only let her come up for air when his own supply of air was gone. He'd promised her he'd never confront her about moving to the country again, and he wouldn't unless he could come up with a compromise. There had to be a compromise out there, and he was determined to find it.

The newness and excitement of Damien's rages soon wore off. No more than a few days had passed before Jennifer felt like strangling him. He defied everyone but Angel. He still did whatever she asked without a qualm. Jennifer sighed wearily as she became embroiled in one more battle of wills, called a cease-fire and went into the kitchen in search of Theresa.

"There are safety standards that deal with the work atmosphere and dangerous noise levels." Theresa stated dryly. "I think all of us should be equipped with ear plugs."

Jennifer sighed, collapsed into a chair and shook her head. "Go out and buy a supply. In fact, buy two pair for me."

"How much longer is this going to go on, Jenny?"

"I don't know," she said with a sigh. "I guess until all his anger is burned up. I sure hope it's soon. I can't take much more of this."

"Why don't you get away for a day?" Theresa suggested as she eyed Jennifer's pale, exhausted face in concern. "Why don't you head up to the construction site and see how everything's going?"

"That sounds wonderful, but I can't today," Jennifer answered, and rested her chin in her palms. "I have a meeting downtown with the mayor. It looks like the money for running this place as a city-funded refuge for runaways is going to be approved, and he wants to talk to me about training the staff."

"You can't take on a training program, Jenny! You've spread yourself as thin as you can."

"I planned on keeping this place open anyway. If I weren't training their staff, I'd be training my own."

"Well, when you talk to the mayor, tell him to pass a law that gives you ten more hours in a day," Theresa grumbled.

"I'll do that." Jennifer chuckled, pushed herself out of her chair and went back to conclude the battle with Damien.

She met with the mayor that afternoon, and they tentatively reached an agreement. The city would rent the current Hamilton House site and pay the salaries of the staff if Jennifer would agree to do the hiring and training. The center would work as a clearing house. Those kids who could be sent home would be sent home, or those kids who were close to majority age would be allowed to stay in the city if they so wished. The remainder would be referred to Jennifer, who'd accept them into the new Hamilton House.

Jennifer returned home elated with the proposition. It was a relief to know that her current site would remain operational without further taxing her schedule, and she'd be able to devote all her time to the kids at the new site.

Theresa gave a pleased nod when Jennifer briefed her on the meeting, and she offered to remain behind long enough to ensure that the program was operational.

Jennifer's professional career was on an upswing. Her personal life was on a downswing. She knew as certainly as Trevor did that once Damien was on his feet, it was the beginning of the end.

Trevor called and informed her that he would be late that night and apologized profusely, almost guiltily. He knew Damien's tantrums were wearing on her and that she was the one getting the brunt of them.

She cradled the phone against her shoulder and smiled at the wall as she talked to him.

"Trevor, I'm not going to let an eight-year-old boy get the best of me."

"I still feel guilty, Jennifer. You're the one who has to face him all day. I'm the one sitting in my office."

"You have lives to save, Trevor. Save them, and let me worry about Damien."

"Jennifer," he sighed, "what are we ever going to do without you?"

"I'll never be completely out of your lives, Trevor. You opened the doors and let me in. You won't get rid of me that easily."

"And what does that mean?"

"That friends never go away, Trevor. Only acquaintances do."

"And what about lovers?"

"If they're really lucky, they become friends."

"If only we could find a way to be together," he began, then sighed wearily. "Forget I said that. If Damien becomes too much to handle this evening, lock him in the bathroom until I come home."

She chuckled and shook her head. "I'd worry that he'd flood the bathroom and drown himself. We'll handle him, Trevor. You don't have to worry."

"I never worry when he's with you, Jennifer."

The evening progressed in blessed peace, and Jennifer sighed with relief when she finally had the entire population of Hamilton House in bed. Trevor still hadn't returned, but she was too exhausted to wait up for him. She crawled between the sheets of her bed, closed her eyes and gave in to sleep.

Trevor crept into her room several hours later and tenderly brushed the hair away from her face. He gazed down at her with a worried frown. Dark circles were beginning to form under her eyes, and she appeared to have lost some weight. He wondered if Damien was becoming too much for her to handle. Maybe he should take some time off. He bent and pressed a butterfly kiss against her forehead so she wouldn't awaken, pulled the covers up beneath her chin and retired to his own room, even though he'd have preferred climbing into bed with her and holding her in his arms.

When Jennifer stumbled downstairs the next morning, Trevor had already left. She gazed disappointedly at the kitchen table, had her morning run-in with Damien and then leaned back in her chair limply when he and Angel finally left for school.

"Jenny, I hate to say this," Theresa began as she refilled Jennifer's coffee cup and then sat down in the chair across from her, "but you look awful."

"I'm so tired." Jennifer rubbed her temples. "I don't know why. I'm getting as much sleep as I normally do."

"Which isn't enough to keep an insect alive, let alone a full-grown human being," Theresa muttered, lifting a piece of toast off the plate on the table and pushing the plate toward Jennifer.

Jennifer wrinkled her nose in distaste as she eyed the bread, and she pushed the plate back toward Theresa. "It's probably all the emotional upheaval with Damien. I wish he'd get through this stage and on to the next one."

"He will when it's time," Theresa responded, frowning at the toast Jennifer had refused. She started to comment on Jennifer's noticeable lack of appetite but seemed to sense that the better part of valor would be to keep her concerns to herself. "Why don't you go up to the construction site today? Get away from here, Jenny. The kids are in school, and Trevor's at the office. I can handle anything that comes up."

"I would like to get away," Jennifer murmured, leaning back to look at the ceiling, "but I must have ten charts to catch up on, a hundred calls to make, and who knows what else."

"Everything will wait until tomorrow, Jenny. Give yourself a day. If you don't, you're going to end up flat on your back or, worse yet, in the hospital."

"If I didn't know better, I'd think you were trying to get rid of me," Jennifer teased.

"How else can I have an orgy?" Theresa questioned blithely as she stood and began to clear the remaining dishes off the table. "Unless you are absolutely determined to destroy my love life, Jennifer, get out of here."

"Well, I'd never want it said that I destroyed another woman's love life." Jennifer laughed, rose and headed for her office and her purse. "I'll be home when you see the whites of my eyes."

"Great. Make it late, and give that construction crew hell for a while. We can all use a rest around here."

Jennifer made the drive to the construction site, slowing as she passed the road where she and Trevor had turned off to park. Her lips curved in a smile. She'd never pass this road that she wouldn't think of him.

When she arrived at the site, her eyes widened in disbelief, and she climbed out of the car and stared ahead of her in awe. No longer were there just gaping holes. Beams were upright, and the roof was going into place. Ron saw her, jumped down and walked toward her, grinning from ear to ear.

"I don't believe this," she said, shaking her head. "Boy, when you guys get to work, you get to work!"

"Once the foundation is poured, we're fast," he replied. "Come on in, and I'll give you a tour."

He helped her up into the framed structure, and they wandered through the massive building. The walls were still open, but as Ron described each room, it came to life in Jennifer's mind. There were tears in her eyes when she finally stood back on the ground and gazed up at what would soon be a dream come true.

This was going to be Hamilton House. Here the kids would be able to run and to roam. Here they'd be free from the provocative promises of the streets and the street's inhabitants. Here they'd be safe and allowed to live and grow.

She turned and made her way to the meadow. She dropped down next to the orange flower and fingered its petals as her eyes drank in the meadow's beauty. Love's Magic Meadow was filled with the colors of the rainbow in its array of wild flowers. Sunlight dappled the grass as it filtered its way through the trees. But today it was a sad smile that curved her lips as she gazed around the peaceful area.

She lay back on the grass, tossed her arms over her head and peered up through the leaves of the giant tree looming above her. Here everything could be made better. Everything but her and Trevor. Tears filled her eyes, but she blinked them away impatiently. In the past few weeks she'd been overly prone to tears, a certain indication of her exhaustion.

She tried to clear her mind and absorb the healing peace of the meadow, but Trevor's image kept forcing its way forward. She muttered a soft curse, sat up and wrapped her arms around her knees.

"What am I going to do about him?" She spoke aloud. "I love him, but I can't change what I am. Is there a way for us to be together? If anyone or anything can tell me, you can. Tell me a way."

But the meadow was silent. She continued to sit there until the sun began to lower and she knew it was time to go home. She forced herself to stand, her questions still unanswered and her heart still aching. Soon Damien would be on his feet. Soon after that, Trevor and his son would move out. Once they were gone, the end would be near at hand. There was so little time left to build up a lifetime of memories.

When she arrived back at Hamilton House and walked through the door, Trevor stood waiting for her in the hall. His mouth was drawn into a grim line, and his face was pale. Jennifer knew instantly that something was wrong, but before she could ask what it was, Theresa stepped out of Jennifer's office, took one look at her and burst into tears.

Since Jennifer had never even seen a tear in Theresa's eyes, she was stunned, and she stared at the woman in disbelief. Finally her gaze shifted back to Trevor.

"What's wrong?" she whispered hoarsely.

Trevor glanced down toward the floor guiltily. "Damien and Angel had a fight."

"And?" she pressed when it was apparent that he was having difficulty continuing.

"It was a . . . bad fight, Jennifer."

"And?" she said again.

"And Angel ran away," he answered wearily. "She's run away, Jenny."

Chapter Eleven

No," Jennifer whispered, shaking her head in denial. "Angel would never run away. She wouldn't do it."

"She did, Jenny." Theresa sniffed.

Jennifer felt her knees giving way, and she leaned back against the door and shook her head again. "Some of the other kids might run away, but not Angel. She'd never run away."

"Jennifer, I am so sorry," Trevor stated, and took a step toward her. "I am just so sorry."

Jennifer's knees buckled, and she slid down the door until she was sitting on the floor. She drew in deep breaths of air, but no matter how hard she breathed, the air wasn't getting into her lungs. She shook her head to keep away the blackness that was threatening to overwhelm her and tried to force herself to think.

"Did she have any money?" she asked weakly.

"I don't know," Theresa answered. "Oh, Lord, Jenny, I feel so bad. If I'd only gotten to the room a second sooner, but the timer had just gone off on the stove and—"

"What did he say to her?" Jennifer interrupted, wondering how she could sound so calm when her heart was beating so frantically. "What did he say to her that would make her run away?"

Trevor stepped forward and knelt on the floor in front of her. He reached out and brushed at the frown lines that marred her brow, but they didn't go away.

"What did he say to her, Trevor?"

"According to some of the kids, they'd just finished his exercises. Angel tried to get him to stand, and he refused to try. She got angry and told him about her sister. She told him that her sister would give anything in the world to walk, and she never would. She told him that if he wouldn't try to walk, then she was going home and she would never see him again."

"Oh, no," Jennifer whispered, and she buried her face in her hands. "That was the last threat he needed. She was all he had to hang on to in a world that was upside down for him. What happened then?"

Trevor could only stare at her in disbelief. He'd wanted to hurl recriminations at his son when he'd heard the story, yet Jennifer immediately defended him. He swallowed the lump in his throat, but he still couldn't find his voice.

Theresa picked up the story where he'd left off. "They started arguing, Jenny. One thing led to another, and finally Damien told her to go home and that he hoped her sister died."

"I have to go find her," Jennifer said, and she tried to push herself to her feet.

"Jennifer, you're shaking like a leaf," Trevor told her as he helped her stand. "Honey, you can't go out there and look for her. Besides, we've already called the police. They're looking for her."

"If she doesn't want to be found, Trevor, the police will never find her," Jennifer told him, gazing up at him with wide, soulful eyes. "A runaway knows how to hide better than anything else. But if anyone can find her, I can. And I have to find her, Trevor. I can't call her family and tell them that I lost her. I just can't do that," she said as the tears finally began to flow.

"Okay, baby," he said, and folded his arms around her. "We'll go look for her. You and I will go look for her."

"How's Damien?" she asked as she tried to pull herself together and managed to at least stop the flow of tears.

"I had to give him a sedative," Trevor answered. "He's asleep, and he'll be asleep for hours."

She nodded, wrapped her hand around the doorknob and pulled open the door. "Let's go find Angel."

Trevor received an education on a side of life he'd never known as Jennifer led him through alleys and slums. They encountered drunks and addicts, criminals and hookers. They wandered through areas that made his stomach revolt. They talked to kids so filthy that he couldn't even distinguish their features. With the kids Jennifer took additional time, handing them cards with the phone number of Hamilton House, assuring them of sanctuary and all but begging them to call.

The hours passed, the night passed and finally the sun rose, but they never found Angel.

"Where do we go now?" he asked wearily when she climbed back into the car after investigating still another alley.

"I don't know," she whispered and leaned her head back against the seat. "I don't where she's gone."

"I'm sure she's all right, Jenny," he said hopefully. "She's been on the streets before. She knows what it's all about."

"I hope you're right," she murmured, unconvinced. "We'd better go home. I have to call her parents."

"Jenny, I am so sorry," he said as he caught her hand and brought it to his lips. "When I think about what Damien's done, I want to—"

"You can't blame Damien, Trevor," she interrupted with a sigh. "He's a boy—a child. He was hurt, and in return he flung the arrow that he knew would hurt the worst. Angel made a threat that he couldn't handle. He struck back out of self-defense."

"How can you defend him, Jenny?"

"Because I've been there, Trevor." She turned defeated hazel eyes in his direction. "When I was almost fourteen, I thought I knew everything there was to know. I was grown up, and no one could tell me anything. I decided I wanted to smoke. I knew my dad would kill me if he caught me, so when we went out on the boat, I snuck down below and had a cigarette. He yelled for me to come up and help him with something, and I threw the cigarette down and stepped on it. Apparently it didn't go out.

"The boat caught on fire, and it spread rapidly. Unfortunately the boat was almost engulfed in flames by the time we spotted the fire. My father bundled me into a life jacket and threw me overboard. He went running back to the radio to send out a distress signal. By the time I came back to the surface, the boat exploded. I watched it blow up, knowing my father was on it."

"Oh, Jenny," Trevor whispered, and reached out to pull her into his arms.

She rested her head against his chest and sighed. "After he died, I was just like Damien. Sometimes I think I sat up nights trying to think up the cruelest things I could say to torment my mother. I hated myself, and I wanted her to hate me. That's all Damien wants. He hates himself, and he wants everyone who loves him to hate him. That way he can be justified in his feelings. Angel was the one person he had to hold on to. She wasn't an adult exhibiting authority; she was just his friend. When she threatened to leave him, he reacted the only way he knew how. With anger."

"When you put it that way, I can see where he's coming from. I haven't given him the support he's needed, have I?"

"Of course you have, Trevor. You've continued to love him despite everything. You haven't done anything wrong. It's me who's failed. I'd hoped that Damien and Angel could help each other, and for a time, they did. I should have seen this coming and been there to stop it. It was only a matter of time before they confronted each other."

"You can't blame yourself, Jenny. You only did what you thought was best."

"And this time my best wasn't good enough." She gazed up at him in despair. "Let's go home, Trevor. I have to call Angel's family."

They returned to Hamilton House in silence. Damien was still under the effects of the sedative Trevor had given him, and Jennifer made the call from the kitchen.

Trevor's heart broke as he watched the tears stream down her face. He knew how she felt. It was the same way he felt when he had to tell a family that a loved one was gone. It never got easier. It only got harder.

When she hung up the phone, he pulled her into his arms and tried to comfort her. When that failed, he tried to convince her to go to bed for some sleep.

She refused and forced herself through the day's activities as if nothing had happened. When Damien awoke, she went to him, shut the door to her office and locked it. Hours passed before it finally opened and a teary but calm Damien wheeled himself out.

Trevor spent some time with his son and then went to speak with Jennifer, but she'd locked the office door and refused to answer his knock. He hoped she'd fallen asleep, but deep inside he knew she hadn't. She was blaming herself for what had happened, and he knew she had to resolve that blame by herself.

The day passed, the evening passed and finally it was time for Damien to go to bed. Trevor didn't bother knocking on the office door, even though he knew Jennifer would now open it. No matter what she was working herself through, she'd open the door for Damien to go to bed. Instead he settled Damien down on the couch in the community room that Angel had been occupying since their arrival and pulled the overstuffed chair next to it so he could hold his son's hand.

He dozed and had no idea what time it was when a constant thudding sound penetrated his sleep-befuddled mind. He forced his eyes open and listened, realizing the thuds were coming from outside. Somehow knowing the sound was Jennifer, he brushed the hair from Damien's forehead, making certain he was still asleep, and then let himself out the front door of Hamilton House.

Jennifer was out on the cracked slab of pavement that served as a basketball court, and he leaned against the building watching her sink basket after basket until her legs were barely able to hold her up. When she stumbled and fell to her knees, he finally went to her.

"You're a little old for skinned knees, Jenny," he said quietly.

"Skinned knees build character," she answered in a voice raw from shed tears.

He dropped to one knee, caught her chin in his hand and raised her head. He sighed when he took note of her tear-ravaged face.

"You've been up almost forty-eight hours, Jenny. It's time you went to sleep."

"I can't sleep," she confessed. "Every time I close my eyes I think of Angel. If I just knew she had some money with her, I could handle this, but I don't know, and it's eating me alive."

"Come on," he whispered. He forced her to her feet and swung her up into his arms.

He carried her into the house and into the community room where Damien still slept. He sat down in the chair and cradled her in his lap. She leaned her head against his chest, and beneath the soothing stroke of his hand against her hair, she finally drifted into a fitful sleep.

The next morning, she and Damien once again locked themselves in her office. Trevor called his own office to ensure that his patients were being handled by his partners and asked that his appointments be rescheduled until further notice. Then he went back to the hallway and leaned against the wall opposite Jennifer's office door. Again Damien came out teary-eyed and quiet, and again Jennifer locked the door behind him.

"I'm worried about her," Theresa stated at lunchtime, and Trevor nodded his agreement.

"I am, too, Theresa, but I don't know what to do. I can't force her into talking to me. She blames herself for all this, and no matter what I say, I'm not going to convince her that she's wrong."

"Why don't you call Edward? Maybe he can help."

Anything was worth a try, and Trevor called the psychiatrist. He briefed Edward on the events. The older man sighed and said that she had to work it out by herself and they should just leave her alone.

Again that night Trevor bedded Damien down on the couch, and again he awoke to the sounds of the basketball striking the cement. Once again he waited until Jennifer had worn herself out and then carried her into the house and held her on his lap until she fell into a fitful sleep. The process repeated itself for another three days.

By that time, the circles beneath Jennifer's eyes made her resemble a raccoon, and it was evident that she was shedding weight at an alarming rate. Trevor tried to talk to her, but she closed her eyes, and he knew she was shutting him out.

He cursed beneath his breath, then prayed that Angel would call. If the girl would only call, Jennifer would stop whipping herself and begin to get some rest. He leaned his head back in the chair, closed his eyes and drifted into sleep with Jennifer on his lap and Damien's hand in his.

The next morning Jennifer awoke abruptly and sat up on Trevor's lap. Her stomach was rolling, and she barely managed to leap to her feet and reach the bath before the bile in her throat came up. Two strong arms wrapped around her and held her as she emptied her stomach.

When she dropped her head weakly against Trevor's arm, he leaned her back against the wall and gently washed her face with a cool washcloth.

"Jenny, you are going to have to start getting some sleep," he chastised quietly. "You're going to make yourself ill."

"I'm all right. Just a touch of the flu," she whispered weakly.

"Oh, Jenny." He sighed, lifted her into his arms and carried her back to the community room.

The next morning was a repeat performance, and when it happened again on the third day, Trevor washed her face, carried her upstairs and laid her on her bed.

"Jenny," he murmured as he caught her hand and brought it to his lips, "when was your last menstrual cycle?"

What he was asking hit her with a jolt, and her eyes snapped open to stare at him almost accusingly. "I'm not."

"Jenny, you didn't answer my question. When?"

"I can't be . . . pregnant," she said hoarsely. "Tom and I tried for years. He was tested, and he was all right, so that meant . . ."

"Jennifer, you know as well as I do that there are many reasons a couple can't conceive, and it doesn't necessarily mean that one or the other is sterile. Now will you please answer my question?"

"But I'm not pregnant!" she exclaimed frantically. "I can't be!"

"It's all right," Trevor soothed, realizing that this sudden surprise on top of everything else would only cause a further shock to her system. He had to get her to calm down and try to rest. Pregnant or not, she had to have some rest. "Don't worry about it, baby. It's all right."

"But . . ."

"Shh," he whispered. "Just try to go to sleep."

"But I have to work with Damien," she said, and she tried to sit up.

Trevor pushed her back gently. "I'll take care of Damien. Just go to sleep. You need to go to sleep."

Almost twenty-four hours had passed when Jennifer finally opened her eyes. Trevor was sitting in the chair beside her bed, and he smiled.

"Hi. How are you feeling?"

"Like Rip Van Winkle."

"It hasn't been quite twenty years." He chuckled.

"You look in awfully good spirits," she told him. "Why didn't you tell me that Damien was standing?"

She flushed guiltily. "It was our secret. He wanted to be able to walk when Angel came back."

Trevor's smile told her he wasn't angry about the deception. "Well, he's traded in his wheelchair for a walker. It's going to take a while before he's without the walker, but we're on our way."

"And Angel?" she questioned hopefully.

"Her parents called yesterday afternoon. She's gone home, Jenny. She's there, and she's safe."

"Oh, Trevor," she sobbed, and shot up into his arms.

He held her tightly while she cried her tears of joy, then he urged her back down on the pillow, brushed the tears from her cheeks and sat on the edge of the bed.

"Now we have to talk about the difficult subject. Jenny, I think you're pregnant."

"No," she whispered, shaking her head against the pillow.

"Jenny, as irresponsible as it was, I didn't use anything, and unless you're on the pill, you didn't use anything, either. Are you on the pill?"

"No, but I can't be pregnant. I told you that Tom and I—"

"And I told you," he interrupted patiently, "that there are many reasons a couple doesn't conceive, and it doesn't necessarily mean that either party is sterile. All the symptoms are there, Jenny. You were extremely tired before Angel ran away—you can't deny that. You even admitted it to Theresa. We both know you've been weepy, and you experienced three days of what looked suspiciously like morning sickness to me. I think you'd better go to the doctor, Jenny, and find out for sure."

"And if I am?" she asked almost fearfully.

"Then you and I are going to have to sit down and have a long talk," he replied, and brushed a soothing hand over her hair.

Despite Trevor's objections, she forced herself out of bed and went downstairs. Damien stood at the foot of the stairs with his walker and smiled at her shyly.

"Dad knows about our secret," he informed her.

"I know, and it's wonderful, Damien," she replied as she wrapped her arms around him and hugged him tight.

"Dad says that when I can walk all by myself he'll take me to see Angel."

Jennifer glanced over her shoulder and smiled at Trevor through her tears. "I think that's wonderful, too, Damien."

He again smiled shyly and said, "I love you, Jenny."

"Oh, Damien," she sobbed, hugging him desperately. "I love you, too."

It was late afternoon when Jennifer finally found the courage to make an appointment with the doctor. They fit her into the schedule for the next morning, and when Trevor offered to go with her, she refused.

She walked out of the doctor's office feeling stunned and disoriented. She wandered the streets for an hour and then made her way to a public telephone. She let out a sigh of relief when Edward said he was free for lunch and agreed to meet her at a restaurant halfway between their two establishments.

She was waiting at their table when he arrived.

"Congratulations, Jenny. I understand Damien Hawke is walking!"

"Yes," she answered and smiled. "He's using a walker, and Trevor promised him that as soon as he can walk on his own, they'll fly to Texas to see Angel."

"I knew I wasn't wrong when I sent him to you, Jenny. I knew if anyone could get him back onto his feet, it would be you."

"Well, a lot of it was just good old-fashioned luck, Edward."

"You're always so quick to turn away from a compliment. You need to learn how to accept them."

"If you say so."

"But Damien isn't why we're having lunch together, is he?" Edward questioned knowingly.

"No." Jennifer sighed, then blurted out, "Edward, I'm pregnant."

He arched a brow, then quietly asked, "Is the baby Trevor's?"

"Yes."

"Does he know?"

"He's the one who figured it out. I didn't think I could . . . well, you know how hard Tom and I tried."

Edward nodded and waved the waitress away as she approached their table. "What are you going to do, Jenny?"

"Do? Keep the baby, of course."

"I knew that," he said with an understanding smile. "I meant about Trevor. You're carrying his child. He isn't going to let you walk away with it without a fight."

"I know." She fingered the napkin beside her plate nervously. "What do you think I should do, Edward?"

"I can't tell you that, and you know it. But if I could, the first question I'd ask you is, do you love him?"

"Yes."

"Is it a forever kind of love?"

She glanced up at him with tear-filled eyes and nodded.

"Then I really think you and Trevor need to talk this out."

"I know that. I also know what he's going to say. He's going to ask me to give up the new site and stay in the city. I can't stay in the city, Edward. Especially now. I want my baby to grow up in the wide open spaces."

He gazed at her thoughtfully. "Wide open spaces are wonderful, Jennifer, but they aren't exactly a replacement for a father's love. And you and I both know that that's one thing your baby will get from Trevor."

"Why does this have to be so hard?" she asked tearfully. "I should be thrilled. I should be screaming from the rooftops with joy, but I'm so confused. I'm going to have to rethink all my plans and all my goals. I'm going to have to consider giving up the site and Love's Magic Meadow, and I've invested so much there, Edward. When I last visited, you wouldn't have believed how much work was already done. By now it's half finished."

"You can't have Trevor *and* Love's Magic Meadow, Jenny, and you know that. The man in me says you should grab Trevor and hold on to him, even if it means giving up Hamilton House. He's a wonderful man, Jenny. He's also a very talented, dedicated healer. To have him move to the country and not practice as a cardiac surgeon would be a criminal waste of talent and a sin against the medical community."

He reached out, caught her hand and gave it a squeeze. "Then I let the professional in me take over, and I see a young woman who also is a very talented, dedicated healer. If she remains here, she'll continue to do wonderful things, but in my heart I know that no matter what she accomplishes here, it could never rival what she could accomplish up there on that land she loves."

He sighed and shook his head. "There is no simple solution, Jennifer. Fact one is that you are pregnant. Fact two is that you know Trevor is going to want to marry you. Fact three is that if you marry him, the two of you are going to have to reach some satisfactory compromise. Fact four is that you will probably be the one doing most of the compromising, since there are no hospital facilities near your new Hamilton House that will allow Trevor to do what he does best—cardiac surgery—and I don't think you can see him doing anything else.

"Talk it out with Trevor, Jennifer, but keep your own happiness in the front of your mind. Find a compromise that will allow you both to have personal and professional satisfaction."

"And if we can't find that compromise?"

"I just pray that you can, Jenny."

Chapter Twelve

It was after midnight, and Trevor was pacing the floor. Jennifer had called Theresa and said she was going to be gone for a day or two, that she needed time away to think. And Trevor knew instinctively that he'd been right. She was pregnant. With his child.

He sighed and ran a hand through his hair. She shouldn't be thinking alone. She should be doing her thinking with him. They should be working together to find a solution to this seemingly unsolvable problem. His temper flared, and he breathed in deeply to control it, but the action did no good. If he could get hold of her right now, he'd turn her over his knee and paddle some sense into her.

He threw himself onto the sofa in the community room and grinned wryly into the dark room. He'd never laid a hand on Damien, no matter how impossible he'd become, and he'd never lay a hand on Jennifer. He sighed, leaned his head back and tried to decide where she was. Then he blinked, and his eyes widened.

"Love's Magic Meadow," he whispered aloud. "Of course that's where she'd go."

He shot up off the sofa, determined to leap into his car and drive up there. Then he sat back down, closed his eyes and shook his head. She wanted some time alone to think, and he'd give her until morning. Then he'd find her, confront her, and, whether she liked it or not, they'd do their thinking together.

Jennifer wandered through the interior of the new Hamilton House and ran her hand along the walls that were roughly finished. When she closed her eyes, she could hear childish laughter filling the rooms. A parade of faces moved through her mind. Kids who'd come and gone at Hamilton House. Kids who were now there. Kids who would follow.

If she gave all this up and stayed in the city, could Trevor possibly be satisfied living in the old Hamilton House? Of course not. Would he want Damien and the child she was carrying growing up in that seedy neighborhood of East Los Angeles? Of course not. It was one thing to adjust to that way of life when he was fighting for Damien's health, but it was quite another to make himself a permanent part of it.

The fluorescent lantern she'd bought in town cast dim shadows over the walls. Shadows that took on monstrous images as she tried to throw herself into Trevor's mind and decide what he'd do and how he'd feel. He was a man accustomed to luxury and wealth, and her current living conditions barely provided the essentials, let alone any of the amenities.

With their combined fortunes they could build a new Hamilton House in the middle of Beverly Hills if they wanted, but somehow she couldn't resolve building a new structure in the city. If it was new, it should be here where it belonged.

Perhaps she could hire and train people to live here and take over the clearinghouse function herself. Theresa could be in charge at this site, and even though she'd miss her, Jennifer knew the woman could and would do a marvelous job.

But even with that solution, she still came back to Trevor. Could he accept living where she was now? Could he survive the topsy-turvy world of a clearinghouse for runaways? It wouldn't even be the same environment that he was used to seeing at Hamilton House. The kids would be transients. Most of them wouldn't remain long enough to bond as the group was now bonded. There'd always be a few kids in permanent residence, of course, but they'd only be biding their time until they reached their majority and moved on.

And then she had to think about Damien and the baby. Damien had fit into the world of Hamilton House. The kids loved him and he loved them. It was like one big happy family. If the place became a clearinghouse, he'd no longer have those friends to play and communicate with, and he'd hardly be able to fill that gap with a baby sister or brother nearly nine years younger than he. By the time the baby was old enough to provide him with companionship, he'd have moved on to more important things, like cars and girls.

And the baby? Did she want to raise a baby in a world with constantly changing faces, or did she want it to grow up in an atmosphere like the one she now shared with her kids?

She released a weary sigh, sat down on the blanket she'd spread across the floor and rested her chin in her hands. The simplest solution, of course, was that she give it all up, marry Trevor and stay home and play mother. The problem was, she could never do that. She let out another weary sigh, lay down on the blanket and closed her eyes. She'd sleep on the matter, and tomorrow she'd visit the meadow. Maybe it could help her find the answer to this problem that seemed to have no answer.

When she opened her eyes the next morning, she was still as confused as when she'd closed them. She turned off the lantern, left the building and made her way to the meadow.

She stepped through the trees, and a serene smile curved her lips as she glanced around her. The meadow never changed. It always looked the same, with its ever-present colorful wild flowers and the warm rays of sunshine bathing them in a golden glow. This was Love's Magic Meadow, where everything could be made better.

Then her eyes darkened with sadness as they settled on the empty spot where the orange flower had always stood. One single orange flower that had seemed to bloom eternally and carried its own secret message of love. Nothing remained forever, she supposed, but it hurt that the orange flower was gone. Tears blurred her vision for a moment, and then her serene smile returned. The orange flower would never be lost. Its roots and its message of love were firmly planted in her soul to be passed on through her to others.

"Hello, Jenny," Trevor said, and her eyes flew around the meadow in search of him. He was seated with his back against a tree trunk, a piece of grass caught between his teeth.

"I didn't see your car."

"I hid it. I wanted to surprise you. I peeked in on you, saw you sleeping on the floor and decided to come up here and wait. You really shouldn't be sleeping on the floor in your condition, should you, Jenny?"

She knew it was his way of asking her to confirm his suspicions, and she sighed and shook her head. "No, Trevor, I suppose I shouldn't."

He pushed to his feet, stuffed his hands into the pockets of his jeans and strolled nonchalantly toward her. When he stood in front of her, he tilted his head to the side and frowned.

"I'm very disappointed in you, Jennifer Anne. You should have come home and talked to me."

"I...needed to think," she whispered, ducking her head and nervously digging the toe of her shoe into the grass.

Trevor watched her actions and couldn't help but smile at her tenderly. "I'll buy that. Did you reach any conclusions?"

"Only that I'm going to be a mother—and I knew that before I came up here."

He caught her chin in his hand and raised her head, gazing deeply into her eyes as if searching for an answer. Then he released her chin and wrapped an arm around her shoulders.

"This really is a beautiful place, Jenny. I sat here for nearly an hour before you joined me. It's peaceful here. It has a special kind of healing property."

"I know that."

"Do you also know how much I love you?"

"Yes," she sighed, and rested her head against his shoulder.

He rested his cheek against the top of her head. "How about telling me all those thousands of thoughts that have been running through your mind since I last saw you? Tell me what you're thinking, Jenny. Tell me your possible solutions and their inherent pitfalls."

"You really do know me too well, Trevor," she complained mildly. "Do you want a one, two, three list?"

"We'll start there."

"Okay. One, we can stay right where we are now. Hamilton House will remain the same, full to the rafters, with kids swinging from them."

"I've thought about that," he responded quietly. "There are a few problems that I can't resolve with that solution. One is that you really do need more room and there's no way we can get that room at your current site. The second is that I really don't want to see my wife and children wandering the streets in that neighborhood, Jenny. It's not very safe."

"I was afraid you'd say that. Unfortunately that shoots down option number two."

"Which was?"

"That I send Theresa and some trained people up here and that we stay where we are and run a clearinghouse for runaways."

"Again we have the neighborhood problem. We'd also have a constant shuffling of people through the house. We'd be raising Damien and the baby among a constant flow of strangers."

"I know."

"Any more solutions?"

"We could build a new Hamilton House in the city."

"But? I hear a big but in there, Jenny."

"I don't think I'd ever be happy with a new, citified Hamilton House. If it's going to be new, I want it here."

"We're already starting to run out of options, aren't we?"

"Yes."

"You could give up Hamilton House, Jenny. You could open up a practice and go to the office every day just as I do."

"I couldn't function like that, Trevor. It's not me. It's not my style of treatment. I wouldn't be happy."

"And you wouldn't be happy just staying at home, either."

"No."

"So we've come full circle." He sighed.

"Not quite."

"You have another option in there?"

"Yes, but it's not going to be one you like."

"Tell me anyway."

"That I come up here just as I planned before I got pregnant, and you stay behind."

"No, Jenny." He pulled away from her. He walked to the center of the meadow and turned to face her, his expression a mixture of love, anger and pain. "I love you, Jenny, and I would have let you go. I wouldn't have tried to hold on to you and force you into a life you didn't want. But everything's changed now. You're carrying my baby, and it has a right to both its parents. I will not let you take my child away from me."

"It's my baby, too, Trevor."

"I realize that, and I know that with me or without me you'd be a wonderful mother and the baby would have the best you had to give. But I think that we both need to stop thinking *my* baby and start thinking *our* baby. Once we do that, maybe we'll come up with a solution to *our* problem."

He started to say more and then cursed softly when a loud whirring overhead interrupted his speech. He stared up at the sky and frowned at the biplane that circled overhead. Once it finally disappeared, he glanced back toward Jennifer.

"When I was sitting up here waiting for you, I realized that I could give up my practice and move with you, Jenny. The problem is, I'm a cardiac surgeon, and there isn't a hospital close by that has the facilities to use my skills. That means I'd have to make a drastic change in my career, and I don't think I could do that. I'm good at what I do, Jenny.

"I also realized that in every solution we have at hand, you're the one doing all the giving up, and that isn't fair to you. What I'd like to do is find a solution that will let us both have what we want. Since we know that's impossible, I'd like to at least find a solution that's a good compromise. Out of all the alternatives, the only really good solution for both of us is a new Hamilton House in the city."

He let out an impatient curse when the plane once again circled overhead.

Jennifer turned away from him and swallowed the lump in her throat. Edward had told her to keep her happiness in mind, and she had to do that. Could she be happy professionally in a new citified Hamilton House? Even more important, would the kids be happy? Would moving them to a better neighborhood remove them from the temptations of the streets?

She was confused and at this moment very unhappy. She loved Trevor, and she was carrying a child that was a result of that love. She wanted this child to have the best, and denying it its father would be denying it part of the best. She glanced up toward the robin's nest and remembered how important her own father had been to her, how essential he'd been in her life. Suddenly she knew the answer. She had to do whatever it took to make her and Trevor and Damien and the baby a family, because no matter how much this land meant to her, it was just that. Land.

The orange flower had taught her that love could make it better, and as long as they shared their love, their life together could not help be anything but better.

She spun around, her eyes now filled with tears of joy and a beatific smile curving her lips. But Trevor had disappeared.

"Trevor?" she said in confusion.

"Over here," his muffled voice responded.

Jennifer stepped through the trees to discover him standing on the outskirts of the meadow, and staring toward the half-completed new building.

"Jennifer, how many acres of land do you have?" he asked when she moved to his side.

"Ten, but that doesn't matter. I've reached a decision, and—"

"Ten acres?" he interrupted, and frowned thoughtfully. "Jennifer, tell me about Tom's death. You said he was killed in a plane crash. How did it happen?"

"How did it happen?" she repeated, now even more confused. "He and a friend had attended a conference and were flying back from San Francisco in a small plane. Apparently the electrical system went out, they got lost in the fog and crashed."

"How do you feel about flying?"

"I'm terrified of flying. Why?"

"Because I think I have a solution that would allow you to keep your new Hamilton House and me my practice, but I don't think you're going to like it."

"What is it?" she asked, holding back the excitement that was suddenly fluttering in her stomach.

"We could build a small runway, and I could buy a plane and learn to fly. Then I could commute back and forth to Los Angeles by air."

"No." she responded immediately, horrified by the suggestion. "Besides, it's not necessary. I've decided that a new citified Hamilton House will be fine."

He glanced toward her, let out a rueful chuckle and wrapped an arm around her, pulling her to his side.

"And I've decided that I'd like to see my children growing up in these wide-open spaces. I think Jennifer, we need to enroll me in flying lessons and you in phobia lessons," he announced. "By the time Hamilton House is ready to move into, I'll have my pilot's license and your phobia will be cured. I'll take another partner into the practice so we can spread out being on call, and when I have to take weekend call, you and the kids can stay in the city with me. That will give our families an opportunity to play grandparents. What do you think?''

"That planes are dangerous," she stated fearfully.

He smiled down at her and then ran his finger down the length of her nose. "So's driving the freeways in Los Angeles. Besides, covering a hundred miles in a plane can be accomplished in no time at all. We can have both worlds, Jenny. We can have them both, have each other and be happy. Really happy, with neither of us having to compromise our careers or our dreams. At least think about it, Jenny."

"I'd be worried sick about you every day," she told him as he led her back into the meadow.

"That just means you'd kiss me all the harder when I got back home, and I certainly wouldn't complain about that," he said as he caught her chin, raised her head and smiled tenderly down at her. "Look around you, Jenny. I'm offering you all this plus every ounce of love in me. We can watch Damien and the baby grow and run through the fields in the sunshine. We can bring those kids of yours up here and give them something special. We can have it all, Jenny. All of it wrapped up in a big red bow. What do you say?"

She stared up at him, worry and confusion flitting across her face. Then she remembered her conversation with Theresa when she'd first confessed to the woman that she loved Trevor. Theresa had asked her if she'd still have married Tom if she'd known what the future held, and she would have.

She could refuse Trevor's offer and move into the seeming safety of the city, but there was no guarantee that he was any safer there than he was in the air. In fact, the only guarantee that anyone had was the moment, and you prayed each day that you'd have enough moments to build a long and happy lifetime.

"I say I love you." She threw her arms around his neck.

"And I love you," he whispered as he hugged her to him tightly. "But that wasn't exactly the answer I was looking for."

"What happens if I fail my phobia lessons?"

He raised his head and grinned. "Then we'll send you to summer school. Maybe even hire you a tutor."

"I really will worry about you every day, Trevor."

"As the days pass without incident, you'll fall into complacency and soon forget that I'm even flying a plane."

"I don't think I'd ever fall into complacency with you around," she said, and lovingly laid her hands against his cheeks. "We're going to have a baby, Trevor."

Violet eyes peered down into hazel ones, sharing secrets that only lovers can share. Trevor scooped her up into his arms, gently placed her on the grass and came down beside her. She parted her lips as if to protest, and his lips swooped down to stop her words.

As they put a seal on their vows of love, Jennifer knew that, even for two dedicated healers destined to travel divergent career paths, love *could* make it better.

*   *   *   *   *

**For the millions who can't read
Give the Gift of Literacy**

One out of five adults in North America
cannot read or write well enough
to fill out a job application
or understand the directions on a bottle of medicine.

**You can change all this by joining the fight
against illiteracy.**

For more information write to:
Contact, Box 81826, Lincoln, Neb. 68501
In the United States, call toll free: 1-800-228-8813

**The only degree you need
is a degree of caring**

LIT-A-1R

It was a misunderstanding that could cost a young woman her virtue, and a notorious rake his heart.

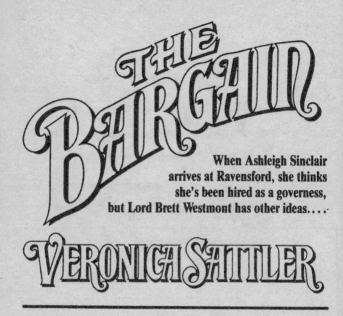

THE BARGAIN

When Ashleigh Sinclair arrives at Ravensford, she thinks she's been hired as a governess, but Lord Brett Westmont has other ideas....

VERONICA SATTLER

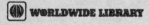

Take 4 Silhouette Desire novels
and a surprise gift

Then preview 6 brand-new Silhouette Desire novels—delivered to your door as soon as they come off the presses! If you decide to keep them, you pay just $2.24 each*—a 10% saving off the retail price, *with no additional charges for postage and handling!*

Silhouette Desire novels are not for everyone. They are written especially for the woman who wants a more satisfying, more deeply involving reading experience. Silhouette Desire novels take you beyond the others.

Start with 4 Silhouette Desire novels and a surprise gift absolutely FREE. They're yours to keep without obligation. You can always return a shipment and cancel at any time.

Simply fill out and return the coupon today!

*$2.25 each plus 69¢ postage and handling per shipment in Canada.

Clip and mail to: Silhouette Books

In U.S.:
901 Fuhrmann Blvd.
P.O. Box 9013
Buffalo, NY 14240-9013

In Canada:
P.O. Box 609
Fort Erie, Ontario
L2A 5X3

YES!   Please rush me 4 free Silhouette Desire novels and my free surprise gift. Then send me 6 Silhouette Desire novels to preview each month as soon as they come off the presses. Bill me at the low price of $2.24 each*—a 10% saving off the retail price. There is no minimum number of books I must purchase. I can always return a shipment and cancel at any time. Even if I never buy another book from Silhouette Desire, the 4 free novels and surprise gift are mine to keep forever.

*$2.25 each plus 69¢ postage and handling per shipment in Canada.

225 BPY BP7F

Name	(please print)	

Address		Apt.

City	State/Prov.	Zip/Postal Code

This offer is limited to one order per household and not valid to present subscribers. Price is subject to change.

D-SUB-1B

Silhouette Special Edition

COMING NEXT MONTH

#403 SANTIAGO HEAT—Linda Shaw
When Deidre Miles crash-landed in steamy Santiago, powerful Francis MacIntire saved her from the clutches of a treacherous military. But what could save her from Francis himself, his tumultuous life and flaming desire?

#404 SOMETIMES A MIRACLE—Jennifer West
Bodyguard Cassandra Burke wistfully dreamed of shining knights on white chargers. Cynical ex-rodeo star Alex Montana had long since turned in his steed. As they braved murder and mayhem together, just who would protect whom?

#405 CONQUER THE MEMORIES—Sandra Dewar
For social worker Carla Foster it was time to face the music. In an adoption dispute, Drake Lanning recognized her for the singer she used to be, and he vowed to learn why she hid her talent...and her heart.

#406 INTO THE SUNSET—Jessica Barkley
Lindsay Jordan wasn't just another city slicker playing cowgirl, no matter what ornery stable manager Nick Leighton said. And despite his sensual persuasion, she wasn't greenhorn enough to think of riding off into the sunset with him!

#407 LONELY AT THE TOP—Bevlyn Marshall
Corporate climber Keely LaRoux wasn't about to let maverick photographer Chuck Dickens impede her progress up the ladder. But traveling together on assignment, the unlikely pair found that business could fast become a dangerously addictive pleasure.

#408 A FAMILY OF TWO—Jude O'Neill
Hotshot producer Gable McCrea wanted newcomer Annabel Porter to direct his latest movie. But what inner demons prompted him to sabotage her work... and her growing love for him?

AVAILABLE THIS MONTH:

ATTRACTIVE, SPACE SAVING BOOK RACK

Display your most prized novels on this handsome and sturdy book rack. The hand-rubbed walnut finish will blend into your library decor with quiet elegance, providing a practical organizer for your favorite hard-or soft-covered books.

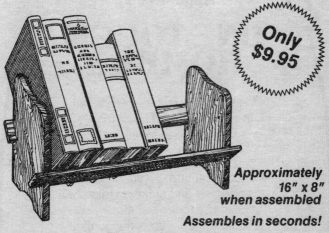

Only $9.95

Approximately 16" x 8" when assembled

Assembles in seconds!

To order, rush your name, address and zip code, along with a check or money order for $10.70* ($9.95 plus 75¢ postage and handling) payable to *Silhouette Books*.

Silhouette Books
Book Rack Offer
901 Fuhrmann Blvd.
P.O. Box 1396
Buffalo, NY 14269-1396

Offer not available in Canada.

*New York and Iowa residents add appropriate sales tax.

BKR-2A